you as a reader. The characters are deeply written, with flawed characteristics that make them seem familiar – like real people that you know and see every day."
    -Ever After Book Reviews

"I dearly loved this romance, and I dearly love this series."
    -Book Chill

"Patience Griffin gets love, loss, and laughter like no other writer of contemporary romance."
    -Grace Burrowes, New York Times bestselling author of the Lonely Lords series and the Windham series

"Patience Griffin, through her writing, draws the reader into life in small town Scotland. Her use of language and descriptive setting had me feel like I was part of the cast."
    -Open Book Society

"Griffin has a knack for creating characters that I find engaging from the opening page. I love the Kilts and Quilts series."
    -The Romance Dish

"I love Patience Griffin!! These Kilts and Quilts books are among my favorites EVER!!!"
    -Margie's Must Reads

"Ms. Griffin paints a vivid picture of Gandiegow with the ever meddling members of the Kilts and Quilts. Fans of Lu-Ann McLane and Fiona Lowe will enjoy The Accidental Scot."
    -Harlequin Junkie

BOOKS by
PATIENCE GRIFFIN

————— ෨෮ —————

KILTS & QUILTS® SERIES:
ROMANTIC WOMEN'S FICTION

#1   *TO SCOTLAND WITH LOVE*

#2   *MEET ME IN SCOTLAND*

#3   *SOME LIKE IT SCOTTISH*

#4   *THE ACCIDENTAL SCOT*

#5   *THE TROUBLE WITH SCOTLAND*

#6   *IT HAPPENED IN SCOTLAND*

#6.5   *THE LAIRD AND I*

#7   *BLAME IT ON SCOTLAND*

#8   *KILT IN SCOTLAND*

————— ෨෮ —————

From the author of It Happened in Scotland

The Laird
and I

A
Kilts & Quilts®
Novel

Patience Griffin

Kilts & Quilts®
PUBLISHING

For Kate

Thank you, cousin, for being my
traveling companion and friend.
Let's always remember the Wallace
and the Bruce and…sheep!
Aye, it was grand!

Pronunciations:

Braw	brave, but also implies fine, splendid, or excellent
Caber	a roughly trimmed tree trunk used in the caber toss in the Scottish Highland games
Céilidh	(KAY-lee)—a party/dance
Kirk	church
Munro	a mountain in Scotland over 3,000 feet tall
Nansaidh	(nan-say)
nighean	(nee-in) means daughter
shite	derogatory term

1

"THIS CAN'T BE!" Sophie wiped the condensation away and pressed closer to the Land Rover's window.

She'd figured Hugh McGillivray's wool mill would be a shed and his house a lean-to. But at the gate entrance, she could see he had a castle! Kilheath Castle—if she was reading the sign correctly. On either side of the entrance stood two snow-dusted watchtowers with the wrought-iron gates hinged open. Quite a sight for a small-town lass who was used to stone cottages and clapboard.

"Sophie? Are ye listening, lass?" her mama said from the front seat of the vehicle.

Her mama wasn't the only one in the car with her. Deydie, the village's matriarch and head quilter, had been lecturing Sophie, too, all the way from Gandiegow, her home on the northeast coast of Scotland.

"Aye, Mama, I'm listening."

Her mother, Annie, turned the car down the long lane leading up to Hugh's home. Conifers, tall and thick, hid the castle, which could be seen only at the bends in the road. Sophie cranked her head this way and that to make out the complete structure.

Apparently, neither her mother nor Deydie were impressed with the grounds or the view around them—they didn't gasp the way Sophie had—but the closer they maneuvered toward Hugh's house—correction, Hugh's *castle*—the more the lecture intensified.

"Make sure to do your bright-light therapy *every day*, nighean," Mama reminded her for the umpteenth time. "None of us want a relapse."

For God's sake, Sophie was twenty-five and able to care for herself. True, she'd suffered from SAD, seasonal affective disorder, her whole life. But now that she'd been diagnosed and treated, she felt so much better. Emma, Gandiegow's therapist, had agreed that Sophie was well enough to venture out and do something on her own...even though it was still January and the days were short. The winter months were no longer painful and full of despair for Sophie, now that she was using her bright-light lamp, which simulated sunshine. She felt fine. Wonderful actually. More like *summer Sophie* than the depressed mess she usually was this time of year.

"I'll be all right, Mama. I promise."

"But at any time, if you need me, just ring me up. I'll come straightaway and cart ye home," Annie said.

"Aye," Deydie chimed in. "Ye'll probably turn tail, but make sure ye have the woollens picked out first. We'll need those for the next quilt retreat."

Deydie made it sound like Sophie wouldn't last the night, but she held her tongue. Deydie was a force to be reckoned with, especially if she had her broom nearby to take a swing at you.

"Ye don't have to do this," Annie said. From this angle Sophie could tell her mama was chewing her lower lip again.

"But I do." Sophie had promised. She'd told Hugh McGillivray by email that she'd housesit for him. She'd also promised Deydie that she'd apprentice with the kiltmaker at Hugh's woollen factory for the next week. "It's all set. The plans are made."

"But…if—" her mother started again.

"Dammit, Annie, stop hovering," Deydie barked. She had a way of knocking you off guard and keeping ye on edge. "The lass needs to put her talents to good use. She's a hell of a stitcher. Ye know why we need her to expand her skills. When I almost didn't get Dominic's kilt in time for Christmas, I made a decision. And when I make a decision, by goodness, it's going to get done—Sophie here, will become Gandiegow's new kiltmaker." The old woman wrenched her head around to bark at Sophie, too.

"Kiltmaking would be one hell of a skill to bring to the table. Maybe run workshops where you can teach the craft to others."

"We'll see." Sophie concentrated on the view instead of the lecture.

"There's no *we'll see* about it, girl." Deydie faced forward and nodded her head with finality. "Ye'll do it."

Sure, Sophie wanted to learn the art of kiltmaking—she was just sick to death of being told what to do.

A second structure came into view, opposite the castle, high on a hill—a ruin. A fence had been placed around the stone fortress, but some of the walls still stood proudly, stretching to the sky. First chance she had, winter or not, Sophie would explore every inch of it. The stones had withstood centuries of dark seasons and needed no bright lights to shore them up.

Deydie harrumphed, her signature sound, a cross between an angry walrus and a beached whale. "Aye, ye'll apprentice with the kiltmaker while ye're housesitting. But just as importantly, we're all counting on ye to use that good eye of yours to find us some nice wool oddments. The wool quilt retreat is in six weeks, and we'll need every remnant you can lay your hands on."

"Fine. I'll pick out some top-quality remnants."

Gandiegow had been building up its reputation as *the* quilting destination in the Highlands. Everyone in the village contributed. Up until now, Sophie had been unable to do much, especially in the winter months, but now that she was better, she was eager to do her part and give back to

Purchase Order #: 09112020
Your order of September 11, 2020 (Order ID 111-4626425-7617062)

Qty.	Item	Item Price	Tot
1	The Laird and I: A Kilts & Quilts(R) novel (Kilts and Quilts) Griffin, Patience --- Paperback **1732068437** 1732068437 9781732068438	$7.99	$7.9

This shipment completes your order.

Subtotal	$7.9
Shipping & Handling	$0.9
Promotional Certificate	-$0.9
Tax Collected	$0.9
Order Total	$8.9
Paid via credit/debit	$41.7

Return or replace your item
Visit Amazon.com/returns

0/U4dhPm6m5/-1 of 1-//MSP5-TWI/sss-us-4/0/0915-02:00/0914-00:23   **M2**

the community.

She didn't say any more to her mother and Deydie, only stared out the window as Hugh's castle grew and the snow-covered gardens came into view.

She'd met Hugh last summer when he came to Gandiegow's midsummer céilidh and dance. Amy, Sophie's good friend and Hugh's cousin, had insisted that she and Hugh were perfect for each other and that dancing at the céilidh would be the ideal time to bring them together. Amy and Hugh may have been raised together by their aunt—as close as any brother and sister—but apparently, Amy didn't know squat about Hugh now that he was grown. He wasn't the fun-loving, happy-go-lucky lad that Amy had described. He'd been an irritatingly handsome brute, who couldn't be bothered to dance with Sophie, even though Amy had insisted.

Sophie had shown him. It had been July, when the days were long with her seasonal depression in remission. She'd exacted revenge by flirting with every eligible man in the room, danced with as many of the fishermen that she could coax out onto the floor, and had finally persuaded Colin Spalding, a local farmer, to walk her home...making sure that Hugh saw that she'd left with another man. But Sophie and Colin were only friends. Besides, it didn't matter; Sophie had never seen Hugh again. Although, she'd thought many times about his handsome face and that look of confusion and pain that had been painted there as she'd sashayed out the door.

Sophie twisted the Munro tartan scarf in her lap. *Thank*

goodness, I won't have to see him now.

Actually, she'd been shocked when Amy had mentioned this housesitting gig. She'd been even more shocked when she'd received an email from Hugh himself. He'd been surprisingly pleasant over the Internet, explaining that he'd be in America for the next week, and *would she mind watching his house for him?* Perfect timing, as far as Sophie was concerned. She was more than ready for an adventure, to do something on her own. A lass of twenty-five needed breathing room from her parents. And her village!

Annie pulled the car to the front of Hugh's home and turned off the engine. She let out a low whistle. "'Tis beautiful."

"It's too big for any one person," Deydie said. "A lass could lose herself in a place like this."

Sophie was counting on it. She was here on a mission to reinvent herself—ready to prove to everyone that she was capable...now that she was doing better.

She pulled out the email with the instructions on it, though she knew every word by heart. "The key is under the small bird statue on the porch."

As she got out, the cold January breeze blew her in the direction of the castle and the many steps that led up to the massive oak double doors. Beside the entry was a stone table, and on top of the table was a small stone bird. But she didn't immediately run up the salted stairs and retrieve the key. Instead, she permitted herself a quick spin to take in the panoramic of the castle, the gardens, the loch, and the hills, before trekking to the back of the vehicle to un-load her luggage.

Annie stood beside the SUV, chewing her lip. Deydie, though, gazed up at the castle. Was the old woman itching to get inside and take a look around? But Sophie wanted this place to herself. Queen of the castle, as it were.

She shivered a little, standing at the bottom of the steps with her luggage around her. "Well, ye better hurry to In-verness, you two, if ye're going to get those supplies be-fore the shops close." And before they all froze to death! Sophie made sure that her voice sounded as chipper and firm as the columns she stood by. "Here, Mama, let me give you a hug goodbye."

Annie's face twisted in conflict.

Separation anxiety. Emma had warned Sophie about it, but encouraged her to not be deterred.

Sophie wrapped her mother in her arms, feeling it, too. That pull to still be the little girl, and at the same time, a woman on her own. "I'll be fine, Mama. I promise."

Deydie tugged on her mother's arm. "We best be get-ting on the road. We'll have the devil of a time making it, especially if there are cattle in the road. *Hairy beasts.*"

Annie let go, but the tears swimming in her eyes had Sophie close to inviting them in for a cuppa. Then the strangest thing happened. Deydie reached out and touched Sophie's cheek, something the tough Scottish woman had never done before. But if Sophie had expected kind words to come from the matriarch's mouth, she was mistaken.

"Pick out some damned good woollens, or else ye'll

be meeting with the business end of me broom when ye get home."

Sophie secured her tartan scarf more firmly around her neck. Deydie's hard words had only made it easier to see them go. As the Land Rover made its way down the drive-way, Sophie didn't budge. As soon as the car was out of sight, she ran up the front steps and pulled the key from under the stone bird.

The email had listed a few chores that were to be done daily, but to a woman who hailed from Gandiegow, the list felt more like a vacation. The first thing was to introduce herself to Hugh's dogs, Scottish deerhounds, who were penned up in the back. However, when she unlocked the door, she was met by the two gentle giants.

"Hey, boys," she said. Hugh had told her they weren't aggressive, which was a blessing since they were almost three feet tall and close to her in weight.

"What are ye doing inside if the master isn't home?"

A sinking feeling came over her. What if she'd gotten the days mixed up? What if Hugh was here? She glanced at the empty driveway. Her mother was gone, and she had no way of getting home. She checked the dates on the email.

"It all looks good." She scratched one of the boys be-hind the ears. "So which one of you is the Wallace and which one of you is the Bruce?" As she read the tags on their collars, she gave them each a hug. "I guess the master decided to leave you inside. Come on. Help me get set-tled."

The dogs followed her as she carried her things into the castle, but she stopped abruptly at the ornately carved woodwork in the entryway. She took it all in—the dark crown molding, the wainscoting, the bannisters of the dual staircase. She reached out to touch the stag carved into the baluster, feeling the wood comfort her as much as any natural light. Expensive-looking vases lined tables down the hallway, and massive painted portraits hung on the walls. The castle was part museum and part home. It was ostentatious, and Sophie loved it.

Hugh had left instructions for her to stay in his room. When she'd responded that she couldn't possibly, he'd insisted. *The view from my room mustn't be missed.*

She dragged her luggage upstairs to the third floor and found his room, dropping her things in the doorway.

"Ohmigod."

The four-poster bed was anchored with what looked like cabers and positioned at an angle so the occupant of the bed could enjoy the magnificent view. Diagonally across the room from the bed were two picture windows that hugged the corner. *If both of the windows were undraped.* She pulled back the curtain to see the sunlight glinting off the snow and ice-covered loch, peaceful and tranquil. The other window framed a Munro, a true Scottish mountain, with its peaks white and tall.

Sophie felt a special connection to all the Munros in Scotland as she was a direct descendent of Sir Hugh Munro who had climbed and categorized most of the elevations. She could almost imagine what this Munro would look like in the spring—lush green and scattered with black-faced sheep grazing at the lower levels.

"Oh, that would be a grand sight to see," she said to the Wallace.

She stepped back and collapsed on the bed. The Wallace and the Bruce jumped up, joining her, making themselves comfortable on the king-sized pillows propped at the head.

"I could get used to living like this!" She centered herself between the dogs, enjoying the incredible view outside. "I'm going to love it here." The Bruce inched closer so he could get his belly rubbed, too. For a few moments, she allowed herself to relax, but only for a few.

"Come on, fellas. Things have to get done. Let's find yere water dishes, and then I'll make myself familiar with the rest of the house."

The dogs followed her back downstairs. Sophie had the place to herself. According to the email, the house staff left early on Saturdays and was off tomorrow, too. This would be her only chance to explore the house without an audience. Come Monday morning, Sophie was expected at the kiltmaker's in Whussendale, the wool village, to begin her apprenticeship, and to meet the other workers at the woollen mill.

She spent the rest of the day in glorious, quiet contentment, without another soul to tell her what to do. In the parlor, she pulled a chair to the window to take advantage of the sunlight and stitched buttons onto the quilted wall-hanging she meant to finish in the next few days. It was her own creation, a depiction of her Gandiegow fishing village as seen from the sea, the buildings stacked against each other. Before the week was out, she would sew on the binding and be done. Another project completed.

Afterward, she wandered into the kitchen for the cabbage and tattie soup which had been left for her in the refrigerator, along with a covered loaf of thick-crusted bread. She fixed a tray and returned to the parlor, turning on all the lights as the winter days were short in the Highlands, the sun fully down by four. She cuddled with the dogs in front of a roaring fire while she ate her dinner.

Very unexpectedly, she felt lonely.

"I've never been away from home before," she said to the dogs beside her.

Black clouds—very familiar and unwelcome—started to cover her. Emma had drilled into her time and time again to be proactive with her depression. As soon as the first wave of despair hit, Sophie was to plug in her therapy lamp.

The dogs followed her to the small writing table as she set up her bright-light lamp and switched it on. She grabbed a tweed fashion magazine off the shelf behind her and sat browsing through it while soaking up the light.

As both dogs lay on the floor beside her, she rubbed them with her socked feet. "Ye two have to keep me from calling home to Mama. She would be nothing but worried and full of instructions for me." The Wallace stood and rested his head in Sophie's lap.

"Ye're both good boys."

After a time, she felt better, and taking the wall-hanging with her, she made her way upstairs with the Wallace and the Bruce following. She draped the Gandiegow Fishing Village quilt over Hugh's rocking chair in the corner. The dogs watched as she unpacked her other things into the three drawers that Hugh had cleared for her. Within a half hour, she had her nightgown on, her teeth brushed, and was tucked under the quilts with the dogs beside her.

Being in an unfamiliar bed should've felt strange. Somehow, though, she was comforted. It was either the dogs keeping her company or Hugh's aftershave, which lingered in the room.

She reached over, flipped off the side lamp, and settled further under the quilts. She was on her own…for the first time in her life. The Wallace scooted closer, cuddling into her back. The Bruce stretched across the bottom of the bed by her feet.

But the darkness and quiet brought back the conversation she'd overheard last night between her parents. How many times over the years had Sophie heard them discussing her depression after she went to bed? This time, though, their concern had been different, and they didn't seem to be keeping their voices hushed as they normally did.

"It's too late for her. She's past her prime," Sophie's father said, much to her dismay. Her da was a good da. Why would he say such a thing?

"It's never too late, if the right one comes along," Annie argued.

"But she's too old. Too bossy. Too set in her ways. No one will want her now." Her da had sighed heavily. *"I know ye like to believe in romantic ideas, luv, but ye need to face facts."*

Annie had agreed, and Sophie had been heartbroken.

But now she was accepting her future. She didn't need love to make her happy. She reached over and gave the Wallace a squeeze, thankful for both canines.

Because the day had been long and the dogs were so warm and reassuring, Sophie fell asleep.

She woke suddenly in the middle of the night, her heart pounding. Had the bed dipped down? There had certainly been some movement. But then she remembered the dogs. She smiled into the darkness, feeling foolish—one of them must've readjusted. But then she heard a deep sigh. A deep, male sigh. *That is definitely no dog.*

"Move over, Wallace," the voice said.

Oh, God, the master is home!

Sophie froze. But her nerves were in a jumble—terrified.

What is Hugh doing home?

Why would he come and get in bed with me after insisting that I sleep here?

A million other questions bombarded her. His aftershave floated her way and hovered, adding to her confusion.

"Walllllace," he said again firmly. She could feel the dog being pushed over. "If ye don't make room for me, ye'll be sleeping with the rams in the sheep shed."

Wallace rose, circled in a C, and plopped down over her legs, trapping her.

Panic had her close to hyperventilating. Without the dog barrier, Hugh could easily stretch out and touch her.

Could she get her feet loose without anyone noticing—man or beast?

For a long time, she didn't move. She lay barely breathing, trying to decipher the different noises in the night. The dogs were both snoring. When she was sure the master had gone to sleep, too, she took her chance.

By millimeters, she pulled her feet free and began to scoot to the edge of the mattress. So slowly in fact, it might turn morning before she made it out. She kept her senses tuned to the opposite side of the bed. Just as she was about to lower her feet to the floor and slip away, a strong hand reached over and gripped her thigh.

"Who are you?" he growled, more feral than any dog in the vicinity. "And why in the deuce are you in my bed?"

She bit her lip, and when she spoke, her words came out in a squeak. "It's me, Sophie."

"Sophie?" He sounded completely clueless. "Sophie, who?"

"Sophie Munro."

As she heard him groping for the lamp on his side of the bed, the hand gripping her thigh held her in place. The light came on.

"Amy's friend?" she added, not certain at this moment if Amy was really her friend or not.

He glared at Sophie as if she was the Loch Ness

Monster.

And that's when the quilt slipped on his side of the bed. The brute was naked.

2

"HOW DID YOU GET IN HERE?" Hugh held on to the woman beside him. It registered that her skin was soft and warm, but he could see only red. "Why are ye in my bed?" He slightly shook her leg.

She pushed at his arm. "Unhand me!"

It was one thing for him to be holding on to her. It was quite another to have her touching him back. He let go and swung his legs over the side of the bed, sitting up and making sure the quilt kept him covered.

She averted her eyes anyway.

"Explain yereself." He noticed his bluidy hounds had ratcheted themselves up against her as if protecting *her from him! Gads!* "Wallace. Bruce. Come." He pointed to the floor beside him.

The Wallace whimpered, and she wrapped her arms around them. "Stop being a bully."

"Good God." He glared at her and then at his animals. "Biscuit?"

Both dogs' ears popped up. They jumped off the bed and ran to him, sitting by his feet at attention.

"Close yere mouth, lassie. In fact, close yere eyes while ye're at it. I'm not decent here, and I'd like to be."

When she turned away from him, he grabbed his boxers off the chair and slipped them on. His dogs were still waiting, so he pulled two biscuits from his jeans pocket. "Here, ye disloyal bastards." For a moment, his eyes searched her backside, trying to outline the body that lay beneath her cotton nightgown. Aye, he remembered Sophie. She was as appealing now as she had been back in the summer. He felt the same instant attraction. Maybe stronger. But he couldn't think about her that way now.

The reflection in the picture windows shifted, catching his attention. Sophie was staring back at him, her mouth shaped into an O. She'd been watching his every move. She seemed particularly interested in his lower half.

"Did ye enjoy the view, lass?"

Her eyes shot up to his. Her teeth caught her bottom lip. For a second, they stared at each other in the reflection, before she averted her gaze. She squared her shoulders and faced him, that exposed look gone.

"I've seen hundreds of men naked."

He grabbed his jeans off the chair and slipped them on.

"Hundreds?"

"Aye." She waved her hand like she was airbrushing him. "Nothing new there." But her cheeks were bright red, and he'd bet his best weaving machine that he'd been her first.

With her facing him, he could now take in the terrain under her shift a bit easier. She was perfectly proportioned, but maybe not as busty as he'd like. With her nipples budding against the fabric of her nightgown, he was more intrigued than he ought to have been.

"Put a robe on," he growled.

She clutched the quilt up to her chin. "I didn't bring one. I was supposed to be here alone."

He snatched up his discarded flannel shirt and tossed it to her. "Here."

She caught it. "Turn around first."

"You just ogled my naked arse, and ye're ordering me to turn around over a couple of perky breasts?"

Goldilocks glared at him, a bit of a stare-down, but he held his ground. In the end, he won, too. She gave him her back while she slipped his shirt over her nightgown.

His shirt swam on her, and the strangest thing happened—something quite uncomfortable shifted in his chest. He had the awful urge to tell her to come closer, stand before him...but not like one of his dogs. He merely wanted her near enough that he could touch her.

Abruptly, his oversized bedroom was much too small and cozy. "Follow me." He only made it one step, before she was clearing her throat with a little 'ahem' to get his attention. He spun back around. "What is it?"

"Could *you* put a robe on?" she said shyly.

She was sweet, and her embarrassment was damned attractive. As if he were a man whose patience had been tested, he shook his head exaggeratedly. "So…a little man chest bothers ye, even after yere hundred naked men and all?"

Her gumption returned. "I've seen more than enough men, thank you very much."

"Aye, me." He opened his armoire and pulled out a T-shirt and slipped it on. "Better?"

"Much," she said. "Come, Wallace. Come, Bruce." She slipped past him and out the door.

His damned hounds lumbered after her bare feet. Those two disloyal bastards needed a long visit at obedience school, at least where it comes to remembering who gives the orders around here. "The upper solarium is to yere right."

For a moment, he stood in his room alone and felt that everything had changed.

He padded into the solarium after her, as bad as his dogs, and found the Wallace and the Bruce beside her with her feet curled under her on the sofa. *Making herself at home.*

She stifled a long yawn.

He stayed standing, hoping to reestablish that he was indeed the master of his castle. "Now, tell me why ye're in my house." *And why you were in my bed.*

She screwed up her face, and the place between her

eyebrows pinched together. "Because you hired me to be here?" Her voice held a heaping dollop of attitude.

"I what?" he said incredulously.

She popped up. "Wait here." The dogs went to follow, but she put her hand out in the *stay* position. A moment later, she was back. She thrust a piece of paper at him. "There. In your own words."

He looked at the email. "What is this?" He scanned all the way down. "I—I…"

"Amnesia?" she provided. She looked quite pleased with herself, perched again on his couch, taking the stance of a vindicated woman. *Vixen.*

Quite deliberately, his eyes bore into her, so she would shrink under his gaze. She didn't. He shook the paper at her. "I've never seen this before in my life."

That did the trick. She withered a bit and uncurled her feet, setting them on the floor. "But—but that means that I'm…"

"Trespassing?" he finished, giving her the smuggest look he could conjure. "Aye."

***

Friggin', frackin', feck. Sophie's mama wouldn't approve of her swearing, not even in her thoughts, but—*damn!* Emma, her therapist, had prepared her for a lot of different scenarios, but being caught in Hugh's bed—with him completely naked—hadn't been one of them. Neither her mama nor Emma had told her how to handle seeing a gorgeous man's *full-monty* reflection in the picture windows either. *Oh, my!* Though there was a chill in the room,

Sophie fanned herself.

Delayed, she jumped to her feet, more embarrassed than she'd been in her whole life. "Sorry." She'd have to pass Hugh to make a run for it, but there was no helping it. She didn't make eye contact, but put her head down and started for the door.

"Sophia."

His deep burr curled and hugged her given name soundly, too intimate for so late at night, and too much for her senses. It made her pause as each syllable registered low in her middle. As she tried to slip by, Hugh grabbed her arm gently.

"Ye needn't tear out in the middle of the night, lass."

His breath hit her cheek. Her arm tingled where he held her. She wanted to go up on tippy-toes and find out what it would be like to kiss him.

He must've read her mind, for he dropped his hand and stepped away.

Great! Rejected once again by the insufferably gorgeous Hugh McGillivray.

"Come." He stepped from the solarium.

For a second, she wondered if he had been speaking only to the dogs, for they trotted after him.

He stuck his head back in. "I mean you, lass."

She followed and found him retrieving an old-fashioned skeleton key from a little basket that hung by the room next to his. For a second, he gazed upon the key and then determinedly shoved it into the opening and turned the lock. He pushed the door wide, flipped on the light, and stood back for her to enter.

The room was large like Hugh's, but not decorated in masculine tones. This room was all pink and floral—rose wallpaper, a gingham bedspread, rose motif pillows, and a matching sage afghan across the bottom of the bed. The Wallace and the Bruce slipped past Sophie and circled the room reverently.

"Whose room is this?"

Her eyes fell to the key grasped in his hand. The key shook with a slight tremor.

"It was my sister's." He frowned like he wanted to back out of the room and pretend he'd never unlocked the door.

Sophie knew all about his sister—falling through the ice on the loch, the drowning—the reason he'd gone to live with Amy and their aunt when he was twelve. His parents had been so distraught that Aunt Davinia had rescued him from his family's grief. Amy had said Hugh took a long time to recover, but he finally learned to laugh again, the two cousins having grand times together.

"Isn't there another room?" Sophie couldn't stay here. "Anywhere will do."

"Nay. After my parents..." he trailed off, but then changed tracks. "All the rooms have been cleared for redecorating. There's not another bed in the house. None, except mine and Chrissa's." His voice caught on his sister's name.

She touched his arm.

He jerked away as if her hand could scorch. "Stay. The

room's just going to waste."

Chrissa's bedroom looked regularly maintained, not a speck of dust anywhere.

Sophie couldn't go back to his warm bed, and she certainly didn't want to sleep in a room that caused him pain.

"Good night," he said abruptly, leaving the key where it sat on the dresser. He was gone.

The Wallace and the Bruce looked conflicted.

"Go on now. Go sleep with the master."

They each gave her one more worried glance and then trotted from the room.

For a long moment, Sophie stood in the middle of the floral paradise—perfectly feminine, perfectly preserved. When the quiet had thoroughly settled over her, she pulled the sage afghan from the bed, left the key on the dresser, and stepped into the hallway. She walked over to Hugh's closed door and laid a hand on it, worrying about the grief that she'd dredged up in him. But she didn't knock, knowing he didn't want comfort.

She sneaked down to the parlor to the loveseat in front of the fireplace. She wished now the dogs had stayed with her for company. When she lay down, the puzzle still remained—Amy had suggested that she housesit, but who had written those emails?

And more important, what would she do now?

***

Morning came too soon. Hugh rolled over and swore, because last night he hadn't slept well. All he wanted to do this morning was to have a lie-in. But it was Sunday.

And light was pouring into his room. "What the…?"

He sat up, remembering…Sophie, this bed. Then it hit him. *The window overlooking the loch is uncovered?* It was never uncovered! Why had Sophie pulled back the drape? The view was more than he could handle. Especially in the dead of winter!

He stomped to the window and yanked the curtain closed. While he was there, he pulled the drape on the Munro as well.

He fell back into bed, but he still had the same problem as he'd had last night. His bed smelled like the woman who slept in the room next to his, and he still didn't know how she'd ended up here. And across the room in his rocking chair was a quilt that was clearly Gandiegow. Had the lass moved in for good?

The Wallace began to whine, and like clockwork, the Bruce started in, too.

"Good God!" The woman and beasts were out to get him. "Can't a man get any rest in his own house?" Maybe he'd let the dogs out and leave them in the cold for a good long while. That would teach them to drag him out of bed early. Even better, maybe he should put them in with Sophie and she could deal with their morning routine.

Hugh rolled out of bed again, went to his bureau, and pulled open the top drawer. He stared in disbelief. Lady things stared back—lacy, sexy bits of intrigue and color. With one index finger, he scooped up a turquoise thong that was erotic to look at, and soft to the touch…and didn't exactly match who he thought Sophie Munro was. He dropped it back into the mix and slammed the drawer shut. He opened the second drawer only to find bras and wool socks. The bras ranged from black to brightly colored, and he slammed that drawer as well.

The Bruce whined loudly this time.

"I'm trying, dammit. I can't verra well take ye out with naked feet." Hugh pulled open the third drawer and found women's jeans on one side and sweaters on the other. "What the hell is going on here? Sophie's certainly made herself at home." Had she decided to move in forever? In the closet, two dresses were hanging, while his shirts had been pushed to one side. He found his socks, skivvies, and other folded clothes thrown into a basket and deposited at the back of the closet. "Good God. Is nothing sacred?" He dug out a pair of socks for himself and quickly dressed. All the while, he groused loud enough to their adjoining wall to make sure his houseguest woke up.

Once in the hallway, he was surprised she hadn't come out to see what the ruckus was all about. Why was the lass still abed? Had she had trouble sleeping, too? He decided to leave her be and deliberately passed her doorway without another glance. Downstairs, the leashes weren't hanging by the back door where he'd left them yesterday. He searched the kitchen first and then went to the parlor to see if Sophie had left them there.

Hugh didn't find the leashes, but found Goldilocks on the loveseat fast asleep. He would've liked to have had a few seconds to gaze upon her longer, but the Bruce and the Wallace wanted her attention. Each of them nudged and licked her face.

"Off with ye," she laughed, coming awake. She sobered quickly when she saw Hugh, tugging the green afghan around her.

"I'm glad ye're awake, Sleeping Beauty. Yere loyal servants would like to relieve themselves, but their leashes have gone missing."

Sophie made an O with her enticing lips and reached around her, shoving her hand into the sofa cushions. "They're right here."

Hugh adjusted the pillows in the wing chair. In this house things were always put back in their place. What he'd seen of Sophie so far screamed disorder. Her tussled hair, her skewed nightdress, and the chaotic emotions she brewed up in him.

He relieved her of the leashes. "The room abovestairs wasn't to yere liking?" He should've been more polite— say good morning first, before starting the interrogation— but the woman had disrupted his sleep.

The hounds jumped up on either side of her, acting as if they were Yorkie pups, trying to crawl into her lap. She hugged them to her.

"Down, you two," he said.

The dogs didn't budge.

Hugh gave the command again, pointing to the floor this time, and they both hopped off and sat in front of him, obediently. Now, if he could only get the woman to obey.

"I suggest while I walk the lads that you toddle upstairs and ready yereself for church."

"Church?"

"Aye. The place with the pews and the preacher." He snapped a leash on each dog. "I don't know what ye heathens do in Gandiegow, but us God-fearing Scots in Whussendale go to church on Sundays."

"Pretty cheeky for this early in the morn, Hugh," she countered, unfolding herself from the sofa.

"On our way to the kirk, we're going to discuss how you came to be in *my* bed."

She momentarily anchored her hands on her hips... until she realized her nightgown wasn't exactly covering her perfect little breasts, and that Hugh was an opportunistic bastard, feasting his eyes upon her.

She snatched up his flannel shirt from the loveseat and huffed from the room. "Ye would think that a man who owned a castle would be more of a gentleman."

"Not when there's such a view to behold. Hurry up now," he called after her. "Dress warmly. We'll leave in the next thirty minutes." He laughed openly as her grumbles continued up two flights of stairs.

The Wallace had wiggled his way under Hugh's hand, and Hugh hadn't even realized the mutt was there. The dog looked up at him with consternation.

"I know, lad. I shouldn't be throwing petrol on the fire." The Bruce head-butted his other hand, wanting attention, too. "But I can't help myself. There's something about that lass when she's throwing flames."

After Hugh's brisk walk with the dogs down the lane and back, he found her in the kitchen. He watched from the doorway as she made tea. She was wearing a vintage wool dress with a million buttons up the front. On her feet she had an old-fashioned pair of lace-up boots. She looked timeless and en vogue—classic, a woman from the past, but one who could also walk the runway of a London wool-revival show. Hell, he could hire her to be one of the lasses to model his woollens. Her blond hair cascaded down one shoulder, making Hugh yearn to wind his hands through her golden waves and hold her in place while he kissed her. *And work at undoing all the buttons of her dress.*

Such impure thoughts, especially before church, had him stepping into the kitchen, making himself known.

"Since you've made yereself at home, did ye make enough for two?"

She went right on rattling the porcelain and rifling his drawers, the epitome of cheek and sass.

"Aye." Finally, she shrugged. "I thought ye might be cold after walking the dogs. Sit yereself down, and I'll pour."

Hugh opened the bread box and pulled out the oat-cakes Mrs. McNabb had left for him. Because things were becoming a little too domesticated and because he needed to remind Sophie that this was his house—*his domain*—he started up the interrogation once again. "Tell me, Sophie Munro, how did all this start? How is it ye've come to take up residence here?"

She ran her thumb over the edge of the silver butter knife. "Amy."

"Amy?" He was getting a small idea of what was going on.

"Aye. She told me ye were needing a house sitter for the next week. She said that ye wanted *me* to do it."

Sophie set his steaming mug in front of him.

"And ye believed her? I barely know you." Which wasn't really true. He knew a lot about Sophie Munro. Amy had tried to set them up last summer, and she'd told Hugh everything there was to know about the lively lass in front of him now. But Hugh hadn't been in any shape to court anyone. Especially one so lovely as she.

"Nay. I didn't believe her. But I received several emails from *you*. I showed you only one last night. I have the rest in my bag. Upstairs." She set the sugar and milk at his elbow, but didn't pour herself a cup. "I'll get my things from yere room when we get back from church."

Damned straight, ye will! It was his house.

She gathered the dog dishes and filled them with water—as if it were *her* house, too.

He ignored the good care she gave his hounds. "Aye. I'd like to read those emails that *I* wrote."

"Oh, ye were kind and charming. Very helpful, ye were. Ye told me where to find the key. Told me to help myself to yere food. Even told me I was to take yere bed. *For the view*."

"Helpful, kind, and charming," he repeated. "And ye believed it? That Amy needs to be turned over my knee for a good spanking."

Sophie set the bowls before the dogs and slung a

dishtowel over her shoulder exactly like his mum used to do. "Don't be angry with Amy. She's a mama now. A good one."

"She certainly thought she had the right to meddle." Both Amy and his aunt.

Sophie glanced at her watch. "You said we had thirty minutes before church. We best be going."

"Aye."

She twisted her watch. "I'll call my mother afterwards to come get me." She looked as if more was bugging her than being sent on a fool's errand. She seemed to be conflicted about going home.

"What's wrong, lass?"

"Ye wouldn't understand."

***

No. A man like Hugh McGillivray wouldn't understand what it was like for Sophie to finally be on her own. Her freedom had lasted less than twenty-four hours. Deydie's veiled prediction that she would turn tail had come true. Sophie couldn't tell the man beside her either. Hugh had been to the far reaches of the world. And Sophie...well, she'd been nowhere.

She grabbed her coat from the hook at the back door, where she'd stowed it yesterday—when she'd pretended this was her house...her castle for the next week. Now, today, she was going home.

She laid her hand on the doorknob and looked back as Hugh downed the rest of his tea. He unfolded himself from the chair and followed her out.

The drive was empty. "Where's yere car? The barn?"

"We'll walk," he said. "It's a mile or so. The weather is only a wee bit chilly."

She marched out, glad she'd put on warm tights with her dress. Hugh walked in silence beside her. Sophie waited for him to question her more about why she was there, but she had to know one thing before returning home.

"This may be too personal, but since *we've already been in bed together*, and I've added to the sights I've seen," she braved, referring to his naked backside, "why didn't you turn the light on when you came to bed last night? It might've clued me in sooner that you were there and vice versa."

He gazed off in the distance as if the answer lay beyond the Munro. "It's my habit." He seemed closed on the subject. But a moment later, he was asking a question of her. "Is there some reason why you don't want to go home?"

Sophie couldn't tell him the complete truth, but she could share a sliver of it. "Ye've made arrangements for me to apprentice with yere head kiltmaker for the next week. Or whoever sent those emails did." Then reality hit. "Or maybe the phantom emailer was pulling the sheep's wool over my eyes on that, too."

"We'll find out soon enough. Willoughby will be at the kirk. He's been at McGillivray's House of Woollens since the day he was born, and he's at least eighty years old, if he's a day."

One thing would be cleared up soon.

"Why else don't you want to go home?"

She kicked a loose rock. She wasn't willing to confess how being here was an adventure for her. He would laugh at her inexperience. But she could tell him about the task she'd been given. "You remember Deydie from when ye came to Gandiegow? The head quilter?"

"Aye. The crotchety ol' bat."

"She's not that bad. Deydie has a good heart, but comes off as tough as an old sailor and crusty as a barnacle."

"I only remember she gave me an earful about Amy. That I should do better about staying in touch, that family was more important than any business I had to run."

"Sounds like Deydie." Sophie envied the geese flying overhead. They were free to see the world with no one telling them what to do. "Well, Deydie's the one who wants me to take up kiltmaking. I can't stress to ye enough how much I don't want to disappoint *her*."

Hugh glanced over, as if to see if she was telling the truth. "And the rest of it?"

Not all of it, but some. "Deydie is also counting on me to come home with some woollen remnants, whatever quality wool piece you can spare. Gandiegow's Kilts and Quilts is running its first-ever wool quilt retreat in six weeks."

"We have plenty of oddments that should work." Hugh took her arm and guided her around a frozen puddle.

His grip was comforting, and she had the urge to lean

into him. For a moment, she forgot what they were talking about.

"I can pick you out some nice pieces before you go." His words snapped her back to the conversation.

"Oh, no. I'm supposed to do the choosing!" She had to be the one to do it. With kiltmaking off the table, the haul of remnants was the only way to contribute to Gandiegow now. And by God, she would do it.

At the Y in the road, Hugh changed the subject.

"There." He pointed down the lane to a group of five or so quaint stone buildings. One of them had a water-wheel. A little bridge was positioned over a stream with two cottages on the other side. "That's the wool mill. Of course, those two cottages over there belong to Willoughby and Magnus."

Hugh turned in the opposite direction. "The kirk is this way."

Sure enough, the church was down the road, with a small town beyond. The church was made of whitewashed stone and had a gray slate roof. Around the perimeter was a fenced-in cemetery with ancient headstones. The building looked older than the Munro behind it.

Hugh glanced down at her, and once again, Sophie was caught off guard at how masculine and beautiful the man could be. She shivered.

"Ye're freezing," he said, mistaking her reaction for chilliness. He put his hand on her back and hurried her along. "I should've brought the car."

"I'm fine," she argued, but only halfheartedly. She felt

right toasty with his hand firmly on her back. Luckily for her, he kept it there the rest of the way.

As they entered the building, the locals turned to stare—an elderly couple with matching Buchanan plaid scarves, a young mother with a babe propped on her hip, and two matronly women. All were gape-mouthed. Hugh dropped his hand and nodded to each one, almost as if he was daring them to ask what he was doing with the female beside him.

"There's Willoughby and Magnus," he said. "The wool brothers."

Sophie didn't get a chance to ask him what he meant as he ushered her to them. The two men stood four feet apart and were indeed prehistoric. They both had bushy white hair, slight paunches at their middles, and frowns on their faces.

Hugh leaned down and spoke conspiratorially in her ear. "They're feuding again. I'll introduce ye to Willoughby first. Magnus will have to wait."

As they approached, the taller of the two pointed at Sophie. "Is this her then, Laird?"

"Aye. Sophie, this is Willoughby, our master kilt-maker." Hugh studied the old man's face. "Then ye do know that she's come to apprentice with you?"

So he hadn't believed her after all? Sophie's blood began to boil. She was not one to lie and connive.

Willoughby looked as if the younger man had grown a horn from the middle of his head. "Of course, I know she's come to apprentice. Ye make me use that blasted computer, and I read yere blasted email on the matter." He huffed as if a shovel had been placed in his hands and he'd been forced to do hard labor. "She's to be here for the next week. Ye told me to clear my schedule to teach her everything I know." The old man shook his head and grumbled, "It'd take more than a week, a lifetime perhaps."

Hugh turned to Sophie and began unwinding her scarf from around her neck. "Ye're staying. Don't call home."

Before she could process his words—she was pretty damned distracted by him removing her scarf—old man Willoughby jabbed a finger in her face.

"Tomorrow morning, be on time," the kiltmaker said. "If ye're not, ye won't be apprenticing with me. Do ye hear me, girl?" He was near to shouting.

"Good God," his brother grumbled from four feet away. "The dead heard ye in the churchyard and beyond."

Willoughby glared at him.

"Aye. I'll be there," Sophie assured him. "On time, too."

"Good." Willoughby left them.

Sophie grabbed Hugh's arm and dragged him to the stained-glass window of Saint Columba. "I'm angry."

"So I see."

"Did ye think I'd made everything up? That I had faked the emails?" She lowered her voice to a hiss. "I'm not so hard up to do all of it just to get into *yere* bed?"

A harrumph shot up from behind her. She turned to see a sour-faced woman wrapped in a wool coat the same color as sheep dung.

Sophie turned red, but she still had more to say to Hugh, so she pulled him closer. "Believe me…what I saw wasn't worth my time."

The Laird wasn't affected in the least. In fact, he made matters worse by running his hand down her arm like they were lovers. "Darling, don't say such hurtful things. I thought ye liked my naked arse."

The eavesdropping battle-ax was clearly scandalized, her mouth falling open before she hurried away into the chapel, looking ready to burst with gossip.

"Just like that," Sophie said. "Ye'd ruin yere reputation."

"Aye. Just like that. That old woman is Nansaidh. She's been wanting dirt on me for years because I wouldn't walk out with her granddaughter. I think we're finally even. I've made her happier than the woolgatherer on sheep-shearing day."

Sure enough, Nansaidh was nattering away with woman after woman, pointing to the Laird in the Narthex, most certainly filling their ears full of how the lord of the manor had fallen.

Sophie perched her hands on her hips. "What of my reputation?"

Hugh winked at her. "What's one more naked arse when ye've already seen so many?"

"Ye're insufferable."

He slipped an arm around her and kissed the top of her head.

Sophie couldn't move. She couldn't think. She thought

she might melt away right there within the walls of the church.

"Stay at my house and apprentice with Willoughby for the next week," he said into her hair. "If ye can stand him that long."

"How am I going to stand *you*?"

He laughed and toyed with a lock of her mane. "That's not what we're debating here. What do ye say, lass?"

She leaned back and stared up into his clear brown eyes. Eyes that had depth to them. Solid, like oak.

The church door opened, and he dropped the bit of her hair that he held.

The newcomer came straight to them. Sophie knew her—Amy's aunt. Hugh's aunt, too. *Aunt Davinia*.

"It wouldn't be right to stay with ye at yere house," Sophie said before Aunt Davinia reached them. "Not all alone."

Aunt Davinia gave her a sly smile and then beamed at Hugh. The older woman was aging wonderfully. "What's this all about?" she asked innocently. Aunt Davinia gave Sophie a kiss on the cheek. "It's good to see you again, dear. Now, tell Aunt Davinia why ye're frowning."

Hugh shook his head at his aunt, so Sophie answered.

"I'm here to apprentice with the kiltmaker. But I thought I would be at Kilheath Castle alone. I'm not the type of lass to plant myself in a man's home, especially one I'm not married to." Besides, as Sophie's parents had made clear—she wasn't marriage material anyway.

Aunt Davinia patted Hugh's arm. "Ye better hold on

to this one, laddie. The rest of the world is shacking up at every opportunity." She grabbed Sophie's hand and placed it in Hugh's. "But this lass, my dear boy, has moral fiber."

Sophie was still stuck on her words. *Ye better hold on to this one.* Then the heat of his hand and the satisfying, steady grip of it made her feel a little dizzy.

Hugh dropped her hand and then wheeled on his relation. "Auntie, ye wouldn't know anything about any emails now, would ye? Or perhaps that my clothes were cleared out of my own dresser drawers and shoved in the back of my closet?"

Aunt Davinia waved him off with a laugh. "Ye've always been the one with the outrageous imagination, Hughboy. Now, Sophie, not to worry. I recently moved from Fairge to the dower house on the north end of Hugh's property. I would be right happy to move into the big house for the next week to make things proper for you and my nephew."

Hugh studied the statue of Saint Jude, the patron saint of lost causes. "Then I'll have one of the rooms furnished up for ye."

Who was he speaking to? Aunt Davinia? Did he mean for Sophie to sleep in his sister's room? *Or with him?*

The organist began Pachelbel's Canon in D. Sleeping arrangements would have to wait until after the service.

Aunt Davinia gave Sophie's hand one last squeeze before the older woman hurried into the chapel.

Hugh put his hand to Sophie's back again, but this time

leaned down and spoke in her ear. "Ye'll sit in the family pew with us."

The words were innocent, but the thoughts he conjured up weren't. His warm breath on her neck and ear made her a little wobbly on her feet and filled her with—she hated to admit it—desire. *The devil.*

He grinned at her burning face and then placed a finger on one of her incinerated cheeks. "Do ye need to step outside and cool off first, lass?"

"Nay." She'd just burn in hell for her less-than-pure thoughts—and in church, no less.

3

HUGH SAT THROUGH THE SUNDAY ser-
vice, cognizant of his houseguest next to him. Sophie was as straight as a matchstick. Was she as hy-
peraware of him as he was of her?

After the service, Sophie took off. He hurried out, not
stopping to speak with the pastor or his workers. He
caught up to her just outside the cemetery fence.

"Have ye entered a footrace?" he asked.

She shrugged off the hand he'd put at her back. "Hugh,
if I do stay at Kilheath Castle, I won't be staying in your
sister's room."

"Are ye wanting mine then?" he said with more than a
hint of sarcasm.

"I do love the view."

As far as he was concerned, the view could be dashed. Especially the view of the loch. *Too many memories. Too many regrets.*

She paused before the first sheepgate. "Nay. I don't want yere room either."

A strange feeling came over him. *Disappointment?* He chalked it up to being a blasted male with sex always on his mind.

"Maybe I should stay at the dower house," Sophie offered.

"There's no space for ye," Hugh lied. "You'll stay at Kilheath." *With me.*

"The emails?" she asked, throwing him off guard. "You really think it was Aunt Davinia?"

"Aye, she and Amy must've been in cahoots."

"But why?"

Because *he'd stopped living*—at least, that's what Auntie and Amy had been saying. Since he'd moved back home and taken over McGillivray's House of Woollens, he'd immersed himself in his work. When his parents had died in the auto crash, he'd lost his last chance to make things right between him and Mum and Da.

"I don't know why Amy and Auntie did it," Hugh lied again. "I'll not let ye go home until ye've learned how to make a kilt to Deydie's satisfaction. Plus, I'll make sure ye have a bushel of woollens for Deydie and her quilt retreat."

Sophie touched his arm, pulling him to a stop. As he

looked into her eyes, he seemed to wake up or to come alive again...at least a very little bit. The deadness and coldness that had settled into his chest eased.

"Thank you." She squeezed his arm. "Ye don't know what this means to me."

But he could read the emotions in her eyes. He saw kindness, and trust, and at the place that she tried to hide the most, he saw want and need. Was it for *him*?

"Come," he said. *Enough of these moments.* He steered her toward Kilheath. "Let's find a place to settle ye into my home."

Nothing more was said as they walked back. The sky had turned cloudy and gray. Sophie's mood seemed to have darkened with it. The Wallace and the Bruce met them at the door and followed them into the kitchen. Hugh pulled the plate of pork sandwiches from the refrigerator drawer that Mrs. McNabb had left. When they sat down to eat, Sophie was quiet and distant. He started to say something—anything—to cheer her up, when the sun peeked out from the clouds.

She popped up. "I'm taking the dogs for a walk."

"But you haven't even taken a bite."

"I'm not hungry." But she looked at the sandwich like she was.

"I'll go with you," Hugh offered.

"Nay. Stay here. I'll be out of yere hair, and then you can enjoy yere lunch."

But I like having you around. The thought shocked him.

She reached for the leashes on the hook, and his hounds went nuts, their backsides wagging as if he hadn't just walked them this morning.

She gave the dogs a small smile, a welcome sight after her sullenness of the last half hour or so. "While I'm putting jeans on, can you get the dogs ready? Put their leashes on?"

"Aye."

"Stay." The dogs plopped their hindquarters down, smiling at her as if *she* were the master. "You stay, too, Hugh. I'll be in yere room for only a minute."

He watched her go, his tongue hanging out, just like the dogs'. Nothing like being bossed around by a lovely Scottish lass.

***

Sophie hurried into her jeans, a heavy sweater, and warm boots. The sun could return behind the clouds any second, and she intended to soak up every bit of the natural light while she could. Her therapy lamp did wonders, but real sunlight had a miraculous effect on her mood and well-being. She had felt the doldrums coming on during the church service, and she hoped a few minutes of sunlight would chase them away.

When she got downstairs, Hugh waited at the door. "Are ye sure ye don't want me to come along?"

"I'm sure."

He handed her the leashes and held the door open for her. "Don't be long. A storm is coming. I don't want to come traipsing after ye in the snow." He pointed to the dogs. "Those bluidy bastards have no sense of direction, and their sense of smell is even worse. Don't rely on them to get you home."

The way he said *home* made her feel warm and fluttery. Which was ridiculous.

"I'll be grand," she quipped. "I've got my bearings. We're just going out for a wee stroll in the sun."

Hugh looked up. "Then ye better hurry before yere sun goes behind that big cloud over there."

Sophie, the Wallace, and the Bruce set out. She wanted to stay in the wide open, thinking of heading toward the Munro, but a rabbit moved to the right. The dogs took off, pulling Sophie into the dense woods. They may not have good noses, but there was nothing wrong with their eyesight.

As they pulled her deeper into the forest, she called after them to halt, but the dogs ignored her. After a while, they seemed to have lost the trail completely. When she was able to pull them to a stop, she gave them a stern talking-to, and then realized she didn't know which way was back to the house. She turned in a circle. In the clearing beyond sat a large boulder with the sun shining on it. She took the Wallace and the Bruce and perched on the rock. As soon as she shut her eyes and put her face heavenward, the dogs went crazy, jerking the leashes free from her hand.

"Dammit," she yelled. The rabbit had returned, and the dogs were gone.

No amount of hollering and chasing after them made

them stop either, or let her catch up to them.

Now what was she to do? She should've thought to stick her phone in her pocket. Or even better, she should've accepted Hugh's offer to come along.

And wouldn't he be angry with her for losing his dogs! She trudged into the forest in the direction that the ornery buggers had gone, figuring she'd find them first before making her way back to civilization. The dogs' barks became fainter and fainter, until she didn't hear them at all.

That's when the snow started to fall.

***

Hugh stood at the back door, thinking the lass really should have returned by now. The temperature had plummeted, and the air was heavy with moisture. She was a grown woman, not a little girl. But then it started snowing. Hard. He waited ten more minutes, willing himself not to be anxious, certain she would show herself any second. He had seen her heading toward the Munro, but had forced himself from the window to leave her in peace to walk alone. Thoughts of her stayed behind in the kitchen as if she'd never left him. He wished she hadn't.

"Blast it all!" He grabbed his coat, hat, and gloves and stepped outside. He would ring her neck for making him worry...*about his hounds.*

He started down the path that led up to the Munro until he heard a noise. He turned and saw the Wallace and the Bruce trotting up to him from the opposite direction, dragging their leashes behind them.

Hugh looked beyond, waiting for Sophie to

materialize at the edge of the woods, all the while formulating the lecture he would give her. She didn't appear.

Holy hell. This was why he would never have the responsibility of a family. He'd let his parents down once, and the consequences had been horrific. Images flashed through his brain, but he put them aside.

Where was Sophie? What if she was hurt?

He took off at a run. The dogs thought it was a great game and ran after him. Hugh stopped and grabbed at their leashes, pulling them to him.

"Where is she, lads? Where did ye leave *yere lady*?" His voice sounded a little frantic to his own ears.

The Bruce whined, but the Wallace's ear perked up. They were a couple of worthless hounds, but something had gotten into the Wallace.

"Can ye take me to her? Can ye remember where ye left her?" Hugh rubbed his head. "Show me."

The snow was coming down almost sideways now, working itself into a whiteout. He prayed to God that Sophie was okay. And if she wasn't, he was going to kill her!

The dogs led him deep into the woods, and Hugh was starting to worry that he himself might get lost with the weather the way it was. But when they came upon the clearing with the boulder, he knew his exact location. The problem was, he didn't know hers!

A hint of burning wood hit his senses. He looked skyward for smoke but could see only snow. The smoke had to be coming from the crofter's cabin on the other side of the clearing. The cabin that he and Amy had played in as children…their make-believe castle.

He put his head down and started plowing in the direction of the cabin, praying Sophie was there, safe and sound.

As he got close, the dogs began barking and dragging him along. When he stepped onto the porch, the door flew open, and the dogs barreled past her, leaving a shocked and relieved Sophie in their wake.

He stepped in and slammed the door behind him. "Thank God! You worried the hell out me!"

"Hugh," she said on a breath.

He didn't think—he couldn't, his relief was so great. He tracked her down, like an animal on the scent, leaned her up against the wall, and kissed her, punishing her—most specifically her lips—for upsetting him.

Kissing calmed him. Soothed him. *Made him harder than the boulder in the clearing.*

He was covered in snow from head to foot, but Sophie wrapped her arms around his cold body anyway and kissed him back—hard.

"God, Sophie," he growled as he pulled away, but only far enough to tug at the neck of her sweater so he could kiss her there. "Why would ye do that to me, lass?"

She moaned, dropping her head to the side as he kissed the base of her throat. "I got lost."

He looked into her eyes. "Don't do it again."

"Don't kiss you again?"

"No." He chuckled. "I'm not daft." He liked that he could kiss her until she was foggy. He pushed her blond hair back from her face and gave her one more quick kiss on the lips.

Things started registering around him. The smell of bacon reached his nose. No, canned ham. She'd made use of the provisions that he kept at these outlying crofters' cottages.

His clothes were wet, and he'd soaked her while forcing his torrid kisses on her. *But she'd kissed him back!*

The Bruce and the Wallace had stretched out on the twin bed, making themselves at home, soaking it as well.

"Down, ye fools," he growled at them.

They slunk off the bed.

Sophie stared at the bed, too. Was she also imagining what she and Hugh might do there? He sure as hell was!

Maybe it was just as well that the hounds had ruined the bedding. Hugh wouldn't make Sophie lie on a damp bed while he drove himself into her.

"The food smells good," he said awkwardly. He stood by the fire, his clothes and boots dripping all over the floor.

"Get out of yere things," she said matter-of-factly. "Ye'll catch yere death. I'll make ye a cup of tea."

He wondered irrationally if she wanted him to strip down to his nothings, how she'd seen him last night in his bedroom. *Nah, probably not.*

"There should be whisky here somewhere." He shrugged off his snow-covered coat and hung it on the back of the chair. He dragged the chair in front of the fire.

The cabin was small with the four of them in the one

room. The more he stared at Sophie, the less he could breathe. At the same time, all her bustling around and taking care of things made it all seem pretty damn cozy.

As Sophie made a plate of ham and beans, the Wallace and the Bruce put their noses in the air, sniffing.

"It's not for ye." Though the Wallace had known where to find her. "Come here, boy." Hugh dug in his pocket and pulled out a dog biscuit, patting the dog firmly when he came to get his treat. "Ye did good."

Because the Bruce never missed out on goodies, he nosed his way between them, and he got a biscuit, too.

"Come sit at the table," Sophie ordered with her still-swollen lips. As if for proof, she put a finger to the bottom one, rubbing it.

"Let me get the dogs' food first," Hugh said. "I've got a container under the counter."

He had to pass by her on his way. It took everything in him not to pull her into his arms again…and maybe not stop this time.

After he took care of the dogs, he joined her by the hearth, taking a bite of ham. He was warming up and couldn't completely credit the fire.

"You scared the shite out of me," he said as way of conversation. Better to be angry than to be drawn to her. "Why would ye head off into the woods?"

"Like I had a choice in the matter." She nodded to his hounds. "Yere beasts saw a rabbit they took a liking to."

"Well, ye should've agreed to have me come along."

"Aye." She poked the fire as if she didn't want to meet

his eyes. "Hugh? Last summer, why wouldn't ye dance with me at the céilidh? Why did ye ignore me so thoroughly?"

The question caught him off guard. But turnabout was fair play. He'd caught her off guard when he'd kissed her a bit ago. *He'd like to do it again.* Instead, he faced her, the firelight catching the blue of her eyes. He could make out the old hurt in the depths of them, and he felt bad for it.

He pushed back her hair and hoped she could see the earnestness of what he felt. "Aw, lass, last summer, didn't ye know? Ye took my breath away. But my life wasn't my own. It still isn't. My parents had died in the crash a month before, and I had only just moved home to take over the wool business. I was half-dead inside, and ye had too much life for me."

Aye, even now.

She laid a hand on his arm, as if steadying him. "I'm going to finish eating, and then I have to get back to the big house."

She'd knocked him off-balance again with her statement…another non sequitur.

"Sophie, we can't go anywhere. It's a blizzard. We'll have to wait out the storm." Couldn't she see that? "Tomorrow morning will be soon enough. We'll need the light to see our way home."

She pulled back the curtain and gazed outside. "You don't understand. I need *the light* now."

He placed a hand on her shoulder. "We have the fire.

There should be a torch or two somewhere and new batteries in the cabinet. I know there are candles. We'll have enough light." Was she as scared of the dark as he'd been as a child? "Ye're safe with me, lass."

"Ye're not the problem." She yanked the damp quilt off the bed and hung it over the second chair back. "I am."

***

"What?" Hugh looked at Sophie as if she'd gone mental.

Which was pretty spot-on. How could she tell Hugh about her disorder? She liked him. If she was being honest with herself—which she wasn't—she liked him *a lot*, and had since the moment she'd laid eyes on him last June. She was being ridiculous. She didn't have a future with Hugh, or with any other man, for that matter. Her spinster status had been a foregone conclusion ages ago. *Summer Sophie* had dated, but nothing ever lasted as *Dead-of-Winter Sophie* surfaced in early fall. She'd known her whole life that she'd never be able to marry. She was too messed up to have a relationship. Then her parents confirmed it—too old and bossy—unmarriageable.

"Take me back to the house," she commanded. "Please."

"I don't understand what's going on here. There's nothing wrong with ye," he argued.

For a second, hope flickered inside her that Hugh was blind to her disorder. But it wouldn't do any good if he was. He'd made it clear that he was too busy to be in a relationship. Or maybe he had been making it clear that he didn't want to be in a relationship with her!

It didn't matter. Emma would tell her to be honest. Own her disorder and not be ashamed of it.

Sophie squared her shoulders and looked him in the eye—the best that she could—by cranking her head back.

"You met me in the summer, Hugh, when, yes, I'm full of life." She motioned to the world beyond the cabin. "But we're in the dead of winter now, when, I assure ye, things can be quite the opposite."

"What are ye talking about?" He scanned her from head to toe. "Ye look fine to me. Ye're not sick, are ye?"

"Aye. In a manner of speaking."

She told him all about her disorder. How overwhelming and hopeless life became. How listless she felt. How dressing, hygiene, and proper nutrition became nearly impossible. How even the simple task of getting out of bed didn't seem feasible during the long winter months.

"Ye see, I have to get back to the house," she said, finishing. "I need my light, or I might step back into the darkness."

He took her hand and squeezed. "I told ye, lass, that ye're safe with me. I'll be here to help ye find yere way."

She stepped from him, embarrassed. He was sweet for offering to see her through the sadness, and for a second, she almost believed him. But he was perfect and she was damaged. The hurt bubbled up. "I may've shared my deepest, darkest secret with ye, but I'll not let ye witness *Dead-of-Winter Sophie*." He had pity in his eyes, which only infuriated her. "You and yere perfect six-foot-three, world-traveling, castle-owning and keeper of two lovable dogs *self* can't possibly know what it's like for me." She thought about the small cottage she shared with her parents in Gandiegow. About how her disorder would keep her from having even their small town happiness, or keep her from getting married, and having a family to call her own. "Ye can't possibly know," she repeated sharply.

He grabbed her shoulders. "So ye've cornered the market on pain and suffering."

Because Sophie didn't understand why he was so mad—*she was the one feeling pretty crappy and irrational*—so she stood up to him. "What do you know about not being able to drag yereself out of bed? Or about not having enough energy to care about anything or anybody?" Her voice cracked, but she finished. "Ye can't possibly know."

"Ye're not the only one who is well acquainted with the darker side of life."

"Really?" she said sarcastically.

He gave her shoulders a firm shake. "Do you know what it feels like to be afraid to go to sleep at night? To be so afraid of the dark that ye want to howl at the moon?" He shook her again.

"But ye're so successful." So together. *So Hugh.*

"Come." He pulled the quilt from the chair back as he tugged her toward the bed.

"Whoa. I'm not that kind of girl—I'm not easy." Though she was pretty sure that it wouldn't take many more of his sweltering kisses to change her mind.

"Sit."

The Wallace and the Bruce looked like the master had lost it.

She pulled free. "Do I look like one of yere pets?"

"Sorry. I've been alone with the dogs for too long. Please sit beside me."

Hugh spread the quilt on the bed. "It's all dry now." He glanced at his dogs. "No thanks to you two."

He positioned himself with his back against the wall and patted the spot next to him. "Take a load off, Sophie."

She looked at him skeptically.

"I promise—hands to myself."

"Fine. I'll sit, but only if ye talk to me. I mean, really talk to me. Why would ye ever want to howl at the moon?"

He shook his head.

She folded her arms over her chest, prepared to stand there for the long haul. "Fair's fair, Hugh. I told ye all about me. Now it's your turn."

He sighed resignedly. "I'll only tell ye so you won't feel like ye're the only one who's experienced misery."

She slid in beside him.

He sat silent for so long that she began to wonder if he would speak at all. Finally, he took her hand, looking beyond the wall where the dishes were stacked on the shelf. "As I said…I'm afraid of the dark."

He wore an expression of complete sincerity and seriousness.

He shrugged. "I know it's ridiculous, but it's true. It all started after my sister, well, after her accident."

As encouragement, she rested her other hand over his. "Go on."

"I was eleven when she had her accident. She was a wee bit, only five. I was supposed to be watching her as we played by the loch's edge. Da had warned us about not going out on the loch, as the ice had thinned. Chrissa and I were building a fort out of the new snow. She got bored and wanted to go inside, but I made her stay with me. Mum and Da were busy with the wool mill. I became so entranced with my work of building the fort that I forgot all about her. Until I heard the ice cracking." He winced like he was experiencing it all over again. "I looked up just in time to see her fall through."

"Oh, Hugh." Sophie laid her head on his shoulder, trying to comfort him.

"I didn't even think—I ran out after her. I weighed much more, and the ice gave way underneath me sooner. As I fell in, I kept my eyes on where she'd gone in, but she never came back up, not even once. I was determined to save her and ignored the cold. I put my head in the water and opened my eyes. I thought if I could see her, I could get to her. But I only saw black. No Chrissa, only murky, dark water." He shifted away. "I failed. I was going to join her. Lethargy had set in, and I knew I wouldn't be able to get myself out either."

He paused for a long moment. "My da had seen me from the window. He hadn't seen Chrissa. He yanked me from the loch, giving me a bluidy lecture the whole time for going out on the loch when he told me not to. When I finally said Chrissa's name and pointed to the hole in the center, the lecture stopped. *Everything stopped.* It was as if my da died, too. Mum, also. Life drained from them, and I became afraid of the dark."

Hugh's breathing had become shallow. Sophie bit her lower lip to keep herself from sobbing.

He went on as if he had no choice. "At night, when I shut my eyes, I see Chrissa lost in the murky black waters of the loch. When I sleep, the dark waters haunt me. Did I tell ye I have nightmares, every night?" He looked in her eyes for the answer. "No, of course not. I'm cursed with the bluidy things, but I have taught myself to rein in my fear of the dark. Ye asked me why I dinna turn on the light when coming to bed…it's what I do to show myself that my fear hasn't owned me. I can't stop the nightmares. But I am managing the dark." He raised Sophie's hand to his lips and kissed the back of it. "Now ye know my darkest secret. Ye see, lass, ye're not alone in yere pain."

She shifted toward him and laid her free hand on his cheek, looking into his eyes with her misty ones. "And ye're not alone in yeres."

"I've never talked about it with another soul. Not Amy and not my aunt either."

To have lost a loved one in such a way and to be so tortured tore at Sophie's heart. In a moment of compassion and bravery, she pulled him to her for a tender kiss, giving the light within her to comfort him. She held him tight, willing his pain to be eased. After a moment, she could feel his burden lift a little, and something shifted between them. The kiss became heated—a veritable fire had broken out—and Sophie was comforting Hugh no longer.

She was doing this for herself. She needed Hugh, and she kissed him passionately to let him know how she felt.

So what if her parents said that she'd never find a man? So what if she never had one that would be hers for always? She didn't want to be a virgin for always either. Maybe—just maybe—she could have this man *for tonight*.

4

HUGH LOST HIMSELF IN SOPHIE'S kiss—
in her goodness, in her light, in her comfort. She
handed it all to him with the touch of her lips…he
was overwhelmed. Until he realized what she was doing—
unbuttoning his shirt. And what he was doing—trying to
unzip her jeans.

"Enough," he growled more to himself than to her. He
pulled away. He hadn't told her his story so he could get
down to her intriguing underthings!

"I'm sorry." She looked stricken.

Oh, God! He wrapped his arms around her, speaking
into her hair. "Ye're not the kind of lass who would let a
bastard like me seduce ye," he said thickly. "Let me hold

ye, and let's see if we both can get through this night undamaged."

The dogs came over and plopped themselves close to
the bed in a show of solidarity.

"Okay," she said on a sniffle.

Dammit. He rubbed her arms, and she shivered. "I'm
sorry I made ye cry."

"Ye didn't," she said. "It's just talking about making
it through the night *undamaged*…it's too late. I'm already
damaged, and there's nothing anyone can do about it."

"What are ye talking about, lass?" Had someone phys-
ically hurt her?

"It's this disorder. I'll never have the life that I
dreamed of. I'll never be like the other women in the village."

He gave her a gentle squeeze. "I don't believe that for
a second. Now come, let's see if we can find the cards I
stowed here. We could play a game to while away the
time."

Her hand drifted over his chest in an absent-minded
caress, threatening his few remaining wits.

"What if I told you, Hugh, that kissing you makes me
happy? That yere kisses are as good as lying under a thou-
sand suns?"

Sophie Munro was a minx. No two ways about it.

He pushed her up from the bed, swatting her bottom
gently in the process. "I'd say, I think ye're testing me,
lass. Play some cards with me. I promise, if I see ye're
succumbing to sadness, I'll kiss ye." And the devil take

him, too.

While they sat at the table, playing high-stakes poker with matchsticks, Hugh entertained Sophie with stories of the shenanigans that he and Amy had gotten up to as children. He admitted that he'd had a hard time at first being taken from his home to Aunt Davinia's, because her house had been so lively. Amy was legendary for her nonstop talking. He'd soon settled in at his aunt's, deciding he had the better of it to be away from Kilheath Castle and the constant reminder of the loss of his sister.

After a while, the dogs needed to go outside. Hugh took them, but when he returned, Sophie didn't seem as cheerful as when he'd left.

"How are ye feeling?"

She shrugged.

"Come here, lass."

She stepped into his arms, and he held her.

"Will ye kiss me, Hugh? For the sake of releasing some endorphins?"

"Ye're such a romantic, Sophie Munro."

"Will ye?"

"I promised, didn't I?" He leaned down and kissed her. He meant to be tender and gentle, but she felt so damn good that he let himself go. When her knees buckled, he scooped her into his arms and carried her to the bed. He wouldn't make love to her, but he would do his best to make her feel better.

Before he laid her on the mattress, though, the door flew open. Belatedly, the hounds barked. Sophie squeaked. She tried to wiggle out of his arms, but Hugh held her tighter. Three people rushed in, shaking the snow off their coats and stomping their snow-covered boots all over the cabin floor.

The shorter and oldest of them moved forward, while pushing back the hood of her mackinaw.

"Aunt Davinia?" Hugh gently set Sophie on her feet. "What in the deuce are ye doing here?"

"I thought we were here to save you. We brought both ATVs."

Donal and Fergus, his gardener and his ghillie, stood behind the matriarch, not making eye contact and looking ruddy in the face. Hugh didn't care—*he was going to fire them both!*

Sophie tiptoed behind him to the hearth and busied herself with bolstering the fire.

"Who said that I needed saving?" Hugh asked his meddling aunt.

She raised an eyebrow, something she'd perfected when he was a boy. "From what I'm seeing, I've seriously misjudged the situation." She frowned like she wanted to back out of the door and let them get back to it.

"Oh, good grief! Nothing inappropriate happened." Except if they'd arrived five minutes later, it might have. "Sophie got lost in the woods," Hugh explained. "The Wallace and the Bruce led me here to find her. We thought the weather was too bad to make a go of it on foot tonight."

"Nicely recapped," Auntie said, taking his arm. "Leaving out all the best parts, I see." She leaned in, whispering,

"If ye'd only let me know where ye were and what ye're doing, I would've given ye my blessing." She smiled over at Sophie, then put her focus back on him. "She's a dear." She shook his arm then. "But ye didn't, and ye weren't answering yere mobile. I assumed the worst."

"Then how did you find me?"

"I GPS'ed your phone, darling," making it sound innocent and normal that an elderly aunt knew how to hack a computer.

"I had my phone silenced for church," Hugh explained, wishing he'd remembered to unmute it. What he didn't explain was that since Sophie had stepped into his life…he'd become distracted.

He ran a hand through his hair, deciding his aunt's arrival was for the best. "Sophie, get yere coat. Ye're going home."

Sophie gasped as if he'd jabbed her with a hot poker.

"To Kilheath. Home to Kilheath Castle," he clarified.

"Oh." She frowned at the roaring fire. "But I just stoked it."

Hugh had to agree. She had stoked the flame between them as well, and it would take some time to douse what she'd started.

"Donal, take Miss Munro back with you." Donal seemed the better choice—married to a lovely woman and in his fifties. Fergus, though, was known as somewhat of a ladies' man. "Then come back to get me. I'll stay and put out the fire."

Donal nodded. "Miss, if ye're ready."

Sophie grabbed her coat, not looking at Hugh as she slipped it on. But Hugh saw her red cheeks, which had nothing to do with the fire in the hearth. She looked hell-bent to get out of there.

But he was a bastard.

"Wait up a minute," he said. He retrieved her hat from the table and went to her, leaning over, speaking so quietly that only she could hear. "We'll talk when I get home. There's still the matter of where ye're going to sleep tonight."

***

Sophie didn't need her coat on her way back to Kilheath Castle. Aye, it was still snowing out. Aye, she should've been a Sophie Popsicle riding on the back of the ATV with Donal. But she was so heated up by Hugh's closeness back at the cottage, not to mention his double entendre that she was downright smoldering. And she should be ashamed of herself for *not* feeling bad about it.

She was quite flattered by Hugh's attention, but she couldn't possibly think it meant anything. To be stuck out in the countryside with so few prospects of female companionship had to be awful for a man like him. Before moving back to Whussendale village, Hugh had lived in Edinburgh, a different girl every night, according to Amy. He was simply hard up...which explained his attention to Sophie tonight. Lucky for her, the wool mill was out in the middle of nowhere.

Donal pulled the ATV to the kitchen door and stopped.

"Thank you for the ride back." Sophie climbed off the

vehicle, looking toward the woods as if Hugh might magically appear.

"Don't worry, miss, I'll get the Laird now."

She started to argue with Donal that she wasn't worried about anyone, but the man had taken off already.

Sophie hurried into the mudroom, stripping off her snow-covered coat and kicking off her boots. She wanted to be changed into dry clothes and her things cleared from his room before *the Laird* returned.

She hustled her way through the house, hearing Aunt Davinia come in the back door as well. Sophie didn't stop, climbing the two flights of stairs quickly. She knew she was being ridiculous, but she wanted to be back in the kitchen sipping tea when the master arrived home.

And she wanted to be composed...which she wasn't sure she could pull off just yet.

She peeled off her clothes and put on dry ones, a delayed chill setting in. Or was it nerves? As she opened Hugh's top dresser drawer to unload it, there was a knock at the door.

He can't be home already!

"Let me in, dear." Only Aunt Davinia.

Before Sophie answered, she closed Hugh's drawer, not wanting Davinia to glimpse her underthings.

Aunt Davinia pulled her out into the hallway. "Come downstairs and have a cuppa with me."

"No, thank you." Sophie's things were strewn about Hugh's bedroom. "I best clean this up."

Aunt Davinia shuffled her farther into the hall,

reaching in to close the door. "You can take care of that later."

"But—"

The older woman looped her arm through hers. "Don't argue with Aunt Davinia. You need to warm yere bones."

Sophie allowed herself to be led down the stairs and back to the kitchen. Just as they got settled at the table, the door opened and the dogs rushed in, shaking snow from their massive bodies. Hugh appeared next, windblown, his cheeks alive from the brutal weather, and looking absolutely gorgeous.

Aunt Davinia grabbed another mug, filled it with tea, and thrust it into his hands. "Take Sophie into the parlor, Hugh-boy, and warm her up in front of the fire."

Hugh gave his aunt a pointed look.

"Run along now," the old woman said, while blowing on her tea. "When Auntie is around, ye have to do as she bids."

He sighed as if Sophie was a burden. Was it so terrible that he should sit in the parlor with her? He hadn't thought she was such an inconvenience when they'd been kissing a while ago.

Sophie picked up her mug, hugging it to her body, and huffed from the room.

Hugh was right behind her.

She should go back to his room, pack up her things, and find a corner of the house to call her own tonight. Then tomorrow, she would check around to see if she could stay somewhere—*anywhere*—than Kilheath Castle. She certainly didn't want to put out the Laird!

Sophie marched straight to the parlor's fire, keeping her back to Hugh. She spun around when she heard the pocket doors being pulled closed.

"What are ye doing?"

He stalked toward her, stopping directly in front of her. "Remember? Our private chat?"

Did he mean to pick up where he'd left off with her lips? Her middle warmed, and it had nothing to do with the fire.

She turned around. "I won't be a burden. I'll only stay the night, then tomorrow I'll find somewhere else to stay while I apprentice with Mr. Willoughby."

"Masterson."

"What?"

"Willoughby Masterson." Hugh ran a lock of Sophie's hair between his fingers.

"Oh," she said breathlessly.

"Ye're not a burden."

Heat rolled off him. Her insides were melting, and for a moment, she forgot to be mad at him for treating her like a liability. Instead, she wanted to stand closer to soak him in.

"What did ye want to talk about?" She was out of oxygen.

He looked ready to lean in and take possession of her lips, body, and soul. Sophie came to her senses just in time and moved away.

Hugh stepped closer. "Ye'll sleep in my room

tonight."

She opened her mouth to protest, but he put his hand up.

"Don't argue. I'm the Laird."

"Aye. Ye're the Laird," she agreed. "But this isn't some scene from *Outlander*. Ye can't order me around."

"Sophie, it's the only thing to do. Ye were brought here under false pretenses. Let me fix it."

She studied him for a long moment. He was a decent man who wanted to make things right. Perhaps he didn't see her as a burden after all. She longed to cuddle up to him, to be a comfort. She had her bright-light therapy to help her. What did he have to help him? "What about you?"

"I'll sleep elsewhere." Though his eyes showed more than a hint of apprehension.

If they were still back at the cabin and Aunt Davinia hadn't come to rescue them, Sophie would probably be in Hugh's arms right now, naked, finding out what it was like to be with a man. She fanned herself.

Then she remembered the predicament of where he would bed down for the night. "Where exactly will you sleep?" The loveseat in front of the fire hadn't been all that comfortable last night and she was much shorter than Hugh. "You yereself said that the other rooms weren't made up." That meant that, for tonight, Aunt Davinia wouldn't be in the house either.

"I'll take my sister's room."

"No, you can't."

"I can." Hugh grabbed her hands. "After Chrissa died, I slept on her floor every night until Aunt Davinia came and took me away."

Sophie got the feeling that occupying his sister's room was something Hugh needed to do, and maybe he knew it subconsciously, too. Perhaps sleeping beside his dead sister's bed would help heal him. She wondered what Emma would think about his plan. Would this be therapy for him, like her lamp was for her?

Either way, Sophie could do something for him now. She wrapped comforting arms around him and came to a decision...he wouldn't have to do this alone. She would be there for him, no matter what. She would sleep on the floor beside him tonight.

***

Hugh liked Sophie's arms around him—*verra much*. He liked that she rubbed circles into his back. He liked the warmth of her buried into his chest. He tipped her head back and kissed her, showing her how much he liked...her. She snaked her arms around his neck. She must like him a *little*, too.

As he laid her back on the sofa, she made a soft *hmmm* sound. When he tried to pull away to make sure everything was okay, she tightened her arms around his neck. He ran his hand down the length of her and found the hem of her sweater. Just as he was exploring under her top, searching for skin, the pocket doors opened.

Sophie tried to scramble away from underneath him. He stilled her with his gaze while removing his hands where they shouldn't have been.

"Hugh? Darling?" Aunt Davinia walked farther into the room.

They both sat up—Hugh still held on to Sophie.

"Oh, yes." His aunt pretended to be embarrassed by the debauchery in the parlor. "I see you were telling yere guest good night."

Hugh sighed heavily. "Yes, Auntie? What do ye need?"

"Donal is going to run me back to the dower house for tonight. But, darling, please don't forget to feed yere guest. I believe she's going to need her strength."

Sophie, red-faced, slipped off the couch and went to the writing desk in the corner. A rectangular lamp sat on top. She grabbed a book, sat down, and turned on the lamp.

"Good night, dear." Aunt Davinia, who didn't seem at all surprised to see Sophie in front of the bright light, waved to her.

Sophie glanced up for only a second. "Night, Aunt Davinia."

Hugh should've felt bad for accosting Sophie a moment ago, but he couldn't work up any regret. He wanted to go back to her, rub her back, fondle her hair, or something. He needed to keep touching her, but instead he followed Davinia into the hallway.

"Auntie?" he called.

"Yes, Hugh-boy. What is it?"

"I need to know something. Is there anything else that ye've done? Tell me now if ye and Amy are done conniving."

Aunt Davinia laughed heartily and walked away.

***

Sophie had her eyes glued to some book, but her focus was all on the Laird when he came back into the parlor. He went to a stack of magazines, grabbed one, and stretched out on the loveseat, his legs hanging off. The air was rife with sexual tension, or with Sophie's wishful thinking; it was hard to tell which.

The Wallace and the Bruce wandered into the room and took up residence at her feet. Those two dogs knew how to keep a lass company. Sophie planned to talk to Emma about dogs, wondering if they had the therapeutic qualities that she suspected they had. And maybe ask Emma about kissing. Between the hounds at her feet and Hugh's expert lips, Sophie had been doing remarkably well without her therapy lamp all day.

After a while, Hugh left the room and came back with a tray. He didn't say a word, but set a bowl of leftover soup in front of her, soda bread, and a cup of cocoa, acting like he didn't want to disturb her reading. He ate in front of the fire with the Bruce and the Wallace staring at him—*the beggars*.

The soup, the warm parlor, and the comfortable companionship made Sophie feel at home. She yawned as Hugh cleared her bowl and spoon from the writing desk.

"What say ye, lass? Are ye ready for bed? It's been a long day."

"Aye." She switched off her lamp. "I believe my

lovely trek through the woods has worn me out."

"Come then." He offered his hand. "Let's get ye off to bed."

As she placed her hand in Hugh's, she wondered if he would kiss her good night.

Side by side, they walked up the wide staircase together with the Bruce and the Wallace right on their trail. He didn't stop at his sister's door, but followed her into his room. The dogs jumped on the bed and curled up on either end.

Sophie had forgotten about her clothes strewn all over his floor. While she scooped them up, Hugh came farther into the room. Had he changed his mind about where he was going to sleep? Her stomach came alive with butterflies doing cartwheels. She waited to see if he would pull her into his arms. But he went to his closet, dug around in the bottom, and retrieved blue plaid pajama bottoms.

Oh. But she still had hope. There was still time for him to make some kind of overture.

Instead, he walked to the door. He hesitated as he exited, but didn't look up. "Good night, Sophie." He closed the door behind him.

She felt stupid for thinking he might try to seduce her. She felt even stupider for still hugging her dirty clothes. *Damn him!* She threw her bundle at the hard oak door. The Wallace and the Bruce frowned at her...or at least that's what it looked like.

Well, Hugh may not want to crawl into bed with her...and he may have decided on no more kisses, but he sure as hell wasn't going to keep Sophie Munro from sleeping with the Laird tonight.

5

HUGH CHANGED IN THE LOO down the hall and went back to Chrissa's room. He stood in the doorway for a long moment. He didn't know what had possessed him to give up his own bed and say he would sleep in here. Like a warrior going to battle, he heaved himself over the threshold, shut himself in, and went to Chrissa's closet. He pulled down the stack of quilts that he'd slept on as a grieving lad and made himself a pallet. He didn't want to stop to examine his feelings. He was a grown man now, and he could do this. He shut out the light and lay on the floor next to his dead sister's bed.

He stretched out, looking up at the dark ceiling for a long time, pretty sure that falling asleep would be a futile exercise. He should go downstairs and have a whisky. He could sleep on the damned loveseat like Sophie had done last night. He rolled onto his side.

As if he'd conjured Sophie up, the bedroom door opened and then quietly shut. She tiptoed toward him and softly felt the outline of his back. He didn't speak, anticipating what she would do next, but he got it wrong. She lay down behind him, wrapped one arm around his middle, and curled into his back.

The *spoon.*

Hugh let out the breath he'd been holding. The spoon grabbed the top quilt and hogged the blankets. He laid his hand over hers, squeezed it, and fell fast asleep in her comforting embrace.

***

Sophie woke in the morning, sandwiched between two warm bodies—neither of the bodies were Hugh. His dogs were cuddling her. They must've grabbed their chance when Hugh had gotten up. She couldn't blame the hounds. She'd been pretty brazen herself, having the audacity last night to snuggle up to the Laird.

She wasn't sure he even knew she'd been there. He'd never said a word, but had held her in his sleep while she held him. Even though she'd slept on the floor, she felt rested this morning, thoroughly snuggled, like a well-loved quilt. She stretched, rolled over, and threw her arm over—she had to glance up to see—the Wallace. Neither dog budged. A pair of black hiking boots appeared in her lazy-morning line of sight.

The boots' owner cleared his throat.

She glanced up and saw a kilt—rust-colored with green and blue lines. If the Wallace weren't dead to the world, she'd be able to scoot closer to peer underneath. It would serve the Laird right. He'd tried to cop a feel under her sweater last night. Not that she was complaining or anything.

"Are ye going to lie in all day or are ye going to hurry off to the wool mill before Willoughby locks ye out of his workroom?"

"He wouldn't dare," she said. "I have connections. I know the Laird." She cranked her head a little more to the side, but still couldn't be sure what—if anything—he had on under his kilt.

"Well, lass, now that's where ye're wrong. Willoughby told me not thirty minutes ago that if ye weren't there soon, ye'd be shite out of luck. I may be the Laird of this clan and owner of the wool factory, but Willoughby carries the keys to his own workroom."

"Damn." She shoved at the Wallace, but made no headway, getting only a doggie grunt from him.

"Wallace, move," the master said.

The Wallace slowly rose, took two steps, and collapsed. But it was enough room for Sophie to get to her feet.

She gave the Laird the once-over and then whistled through her teeth. "Why're ye wearing yere colors?"

"It's what I wear to the mill." He tapped his watch. "You have ten minutes, if ye plan to be working there today, too."

She hurried past Hugh. "Fine. Will you drive me? So I won't be late?"

"I'll be waiting downstairs."

Sophie put on a white sweater with her Munro tartan skirt. When she got to the kitchen, Hugh had a cup of tea waiting and a bag in his hand.

"It's yere breakfast. Mrs. McNabb will bring our lunch to us later."

"Thank you." She took the sack and hurried out the door to his Mercedes SUV as the sun was peeking over the horizon.

Hugh drove her to the wool mill while she inhaled her cinnamon raisin scone and scalded her mouth on the tea.

"It's delicious," she said around a bite.

Hugh only nodded. He didn't mention last night, and she didn't either. He pulled up to the building farthest from the road.

"He's in there. If he hasn't locked the door already." Hugh had laughter in his voice, but he gave her an encouraging smile. "Go on now. I'll stop by with yere lunch later. Ye can tell me how it goes."

"Thanks again," she said, feeling reluctant to leave his smile, but pulling herself from the car.

"Sophie?"

"Yes?"

"Good luck!" With his eyes dancing, he toasted her with his travel mug.

Sophie ran inside and met Willoughby at the door.

Sure enough, he had the key in his hand, ready to lock out.

"Ye're late," the old man said.

"No. I'm right on time."

"Well, I didn't think ye'd make it." He sounded disappointed. "I've a lot of work to do. Don't have time for the likes of ye."

Why hadn't she brought an extra scone—some little thing with which to butter up the old man?

"Well, I'm here," she said cheerily. "Ready to make my first kilt."

"Not so fast," Willoughby said. "I'll have to see some of your handiwork first before I'll let ye be touching the tartans with the scissors." With a gnarled hand, he pocketed the key in his old tweed jacket. From inside the coat, he withdrew a thick piece of wool tartan and a needle. He thrust them at her. "Make three evenly spaced pleats."

Sophie claimed a small table and plain ladder-back chair for herself. Willoughby shuffled over to a narrow table that had to be fifteen to twenty feet long. A large bolt of a dark green tartan with muted aqua and royal blue stripes sat at one end.

"Stop staring at me and get busy," he grumbled.

"Aye." *What a cheery instructor.*

Sophie laid out her length of fabric on the table and grabbed the pins off the windowsill. She went to work, marking evenly spaced pleats and sewing them into place. She should've asked Hugh this morning if he'd strip out of his kilt so she could check to see how the stitching was ıe.

She smiled at the image and let her mind wander. How nice it'd been sleeping with Hugh last night. And before that, his nakedness in the reflection of his picture window had been pretty wonderful, too. What an education she'd been getting at Kilheath Castle.

Willoughby coughed. "Are ye done yet? We don't have all day."

Sophie walked her pleats over to him. He scowled at her as he snatched the fabric away, but his expression changed to confusion as he examined the woollen.

"That don't mean a thing," he muttered to himself, shoving the pleated piece back in his inside pocket. "Get up here and start rolling out the tartan. The Laird needs a new kilt. And ye're going to make it." He said it like that would show the new master for off-loading her onto him.

No! She wanted to protest. She didn't trust that her first kilt would be good enough for Hugh. What if she screwed it up?

But if she backed down from this order, Willoughby would throw her out of his workshop for good.

"Fine." She stepped up to the counter. "Eight yards, right?" She began spreading out the wool, wondering if Willoughby was impressed that she knew how much fabric was in a kilt. "I assume this is the McGillivray Hunting tartan."

"Aye." He pointed to a corner where bolts had been stacked. "The *modern* McGillivray Hunting tartan," Willoughby corrected. "Magnus, me brother, finished weaving it yesterday."

She ran her hand over the quality wool. "It's beautiful."

"I'm glad ye can appreciate fine craftsmanship. My brother may be an arse, but he does weave the best tartan in all of Scotland."

His voice held pride, and as he instructed her on how to measure and mark the pleats, his voice became less rough, and she heard the passion for his craft in his words.

At noon, Hugh knocked on the jamb, making Sophie and Willoughby look up from their work.

"Lunch," he said. "Willoughby, do ye want to join us?"

"Nay. I have to complete all the things *yere* lass kept me from this morning."

Sophie ignored that the old man had lumped her and Hugh together with his *yere lass*.

"I'll be back soon," she said.

"Don't hurry," Willoughby answered gruffly. He didn't really look angry with her, now that she was getting to know him.

Hugh grabbed her coat and helped her into it. Sophie savored his closeness, allowing a second to breathe him in. She could pretend for this moment that she was his lass, couldn't she?

He walked her out, and as they made their way through the compound, he pointed out the various buildings of the wool operation, starting with the exhibition hall.

"We're a sheep-to-shawl operation," he said proudly.

"We do sheep-shearing demonstrations here, but mostly the shearing is done at my cousin Ewan's sheep farm down the way."

"Nepotism?" she kidded.

"Aye, I'm happy to say. Most of our families have been here in the village of Whussendale and have been working at McGillivray's House of Woollens from the beginning. And will continue to be here for generations to come, if I have any say about it."

"What about outsiders? Do ye welcome them?" Sophie's village of Gandiegow could be pretty closed-minded when it came to outsiders moving in.

"Absolutely. We're expanding things here. I have visions of Whussendale becoming an artisan community. I've been working to bring in a potter to set up shop here." He pointed to a funny little green building among the stone cottages. "After that, I'd like to see about getting a basket-maker and an artist here as well."

They passed the building with the waterwheel, and he explained how it provided only a fraction of the energy needed. "We rely mostly on conventional electricity. Though, I strive to keep the old ways alive as much as possible. My father and mother worked hard to preserve the Victorian-era wool mill operation, maintain its authenticity. I'm trying to carry on the tradition. That doesn't mean that some modernization hasn't had to take place. We still have to compete to sell our woollens."

They toured several buildings, and Sophie couldn't help but revel when he'd lay his hand at the small of her back and guided her along. Everyplace they went, the Laird gave her a thorough explanation of each process. He was passionate about what he did, and she couldn't imagine that he'd spent so many years away—or that now that he was home that he would ever leave this place again.

They finally made it to his office in the middle of the complex. Once inside, Hugh settled them at a small conference table in the corner, pulling up two chairs. Sophie retrieved warm meat pies and tea from a picnic basket.

"Compliments of Mrs. McNabb," he said.

Would he bring up last night now? She opened her mouth to ask about the sleeping arrangements—if the other bedrooms were being outfitted as they ate—but he jumped in first.

"How are ye getting along with Willoughby?" Hugh asked. "I think he's taken quite a shine to you."

She gave him a half frown. "That's a *shine*?"

"Aye. He actually let ye stay in his workshop, for one thing. It took Mrs. Bates two years to pass his pleat test before he'd let her sew the buckles on his completed kilts. His damned pleat test is the reason I haven't been able to hire someone to take over…someday."

Sophie was getting a clue as to why Willoughby would be reticent to have her or anyone else there. He saw her as a threat. She'd have to assure him that she had no intention of taking his place. She was going home soon.

One week. It just didn't feel like it was long enough.

Hugh's office made an interesting comment on the man who occupied it. Five bolts of various tartans were propped in the corner—from muted hunting plaids to the Royal Stewart tartan. A mound of folders and paperwork sat on his desk. And the man across from her was staring back at her.

"What?" Sophie asked. "Do I have meat pie on my chin?"

"Aye." He reached over and wiped away a bit of gravy from the corner of her mouth. The gesture was very intimate, but not as intimate as what he did next. He stared into her eyes for a long moment.

He broke the spell, looking away. "I have to get back to work. Can ye make it to the workshop on yere own?"

"Certainly."

"I'll leave the auto for ye for later." He tried to hand her the keys.

She waved him off. "I'll walk. 'Tis not that far."

"I'll be here until late," he said. "Don't wait up for me."

"But—"

The phone on the desk rang, and he reached for it. "I have to get this." He turned his back, and their companionable lunch was over.

Sophie grabbed her coat and left. When she got back to the workshop, it was locked. She peeked in the windows, but didn't see the stubborn Willoughby with his key on the other side. She wandered into the building next to the kiltmaker's. Inside, she found what could only be a small café. Three women and two men sat at a table having lunch. One of them was Magnus, Willoughby's brother.

"Excuse me," Sophie said. They'd stopped eating when she'd walked in. "Do you know where Willoughby might be?"

Magnus harrumphed. "Doing a dance with the devil, for all I care."

The oldest woman playfully smacked Magnus's arm. "Don't mind him. They're feuding again."

"Here, come sit with us," said the youngest of the three women. She was dark-haired and petite. She scooted over and made room for Sophie. "We can get Elspeth to ladle up a bowl for ye in the kitchen."

"No, thanks. I already ate." *With the Laird.*

The first woman made the introductions. "I'm Hazel, this is Taffy, and this is Lara, the babe of the group. This one is my husband, Harold, and of course, ye know Mr. Grumpy Pants here, one of the wool brothers. If ye're looking for Willoughby, he probably has gone home for a wee nap."

Magnus harrumphed again and muttered, "Lazy bum."

Taffy rubbed Magnus's arm this time. "Be kind, luv. He's much older than you, and he needs his nap to make it through the afternoon."

First, Sophie really didn't believe that Willoughby could be that much older than Magnus, maybe a year or two. Second, it looked like Taffy had a bit of a crush on the old weaver.

They all chatted for a bit until the young woman piped up. "How about I walk you back?"

Sophie had a feeling that Lara wanted to pump her for

information about why she was here...and with the Laird. The woman seemed so nice that Sophie didn't mind. "Sure."

Lara wiped her mouth and grabbed her coat.

When they got outside and before Lara could get in the first question, Sophie asked her what she did for the wool mill—"I dye the wool"—and kept her talking until they reached the kiltmaker's workshop.

"This is me. Thanks for the company," Sophie said and ducked inside. Unfortunately, Willoughby hadn't taken a long nap and was back at his place, making a kilt out of the Royal Stewart tartan. Mrs. Bates was there, too, sewing on buckles. He gave Sophie a withering glare.

"Sorry, I'm late." It wouldn't be gracious to mention his nap. She got right back to work on the Laird's kilt.

At five o'clock, they cleaned up the shop and Willoughby locked up. It was dark out, but the light was on in Hugh's office as Sophie walked by. When would he make it home?

She began the trek to Kilheath Castle, walking a ways with Hazel, Harold, and Lara, her new acquaintances. By the time Sophie made it to Hugh's home, she was very glad to see the Wallace and the Bruce. She expected to see Hugh's aunt, but Davinia wasn't in the house.

After taking the dogs for a walk, *close to the house this time*, Sophie heated up her dinner. She sat in front of her therapy lamp, eating her haggis stovies while the hounds rested at her feet. She felt good about the day, but one thing nagged at her...when was Hugh getting home?

She pulled out her phone, but Amy hadn't responded yet to her texts or her voicemails. Sophie sent messages to both Emma and her cousin Ramsay—whom she could trust to get it done.

When you see Amy, tell her to call me!

Sophie's eyes began to droop. She and the dogs hauled themselves upstairs. She looked in every bedroom, but found none had been furnished yet, which explained why Davinia hadn't moved in today.

Sophie had two choices: She could pass out in Hugh's bed or sleep in his sister's room. She decided to do both. For now, she and her dog friends would cuddle in the master's bed. Later, when Hugh got home—*if he didn't come crawl into bed with her*—she'd sleep beside him again on the floor.

She changed and snuggled under Hugh's quilt, feeling a little cheated—the Laird hadn't kissed her once today. Interesting how quickly she'd grown accustomed to his lips on hers.

Sophie woke up an hour later to a thump and a litany of swear words in a baritone hiss. *Oops. Maybe she should've picked her things up off the floor before she went to bed.* She expected the bed to dip down like the first night, and she lay there in glorious anticipation. But the bedroom door clicked shut, and she was alone.

In the room next to hers, the Laird was making up his pallet, still cussing on and off. When he grew quiet, Sophie stole out of bed and sneaked in to sleep next to his warm body with her arms wrapped around him.

***

Hugh laid his arm on top of Sophie's and held her hand, not sure why she insisted on torturing him like his. God, didn't she know he'd stayed away tonight on purpose? She was too much for him…he was a man who was half-dead inside. Fortunately, she cuddled his back, instead of slipping into his arms for him to spoon her—or else, Sophie Munro might've had quite a surprise pressing up against her bum.

It took everything in him not to turn and face her, kiss her, and to love her all night long. But he could withstand her time here and keep his lips off her. *Couldn't he?*

Sophie's breathing evened, and Hugh raised her hand to his mouth and kissed it. She sighed in her sleep and pressed her hips into him from behind.

God. She was going to be the end of him!

Hugh had done something for Sophie today. He'd made a call to his friend Liam, his roommate from university, an art dealer now. Liam agreed to overnight a vase that Hugh had admired in his friend's study on his last visit to Perth. Aye, it was impulsive, but Hugh hoped the gift would be a comfort to Sophie when she was gone from here.

For a long time, he lay in her embrace. When he'd gotten home, the first thing he'd done was check the four other bedrooms.

But the furniture hadn't been delivered today as promised. Hugh checked Aunt Davinia's room on the main level, and it was still empty, too. He was getting the stinking suspicion that someone had canceled his order at the furniture store in Inverness.

He shouldn't be surprised that Aunt Davinia had hacked into his home computer again. He'd have to confiscate her key to the castle!

He didn't understand why Davinia and Amy were so hell-bent on finding him a wife. His parents hadn't been particularly happy being married, though maybe he was only remembering the time after Chrissa's accident.

Sophie squeezed his hand in her sleep, and a memory came flooding back. The family had been sitting in their pew at the kirk on a warm Sunday. For once, he and Chrissa were behaving while the pastor droned on. Hugh had looked up to see his parents share a look—*a look of love and connection*. He'd watched as his da had taken his mum's hand, and she'd squeezed it back.

And Hugh remembered how comforted he'd been, how happy.

Grief had a way of masking the nicer emotions, and he'd forgotten how his parents had really loved each other.

Hugh kissed Sophie's hand again. A warmth spread into his chest, and he felt lighter than he had. He closed his eyes and went to sleep, content.

***

The next morning when Sophie awoke, she was alone, and the Laird was gone from the castle. He'd been thoughtful enough to leave her the car, but she walked to the mill instead, as the weather had turned unseasonably warm for the Highlands. She worked with Willoughby, ate lunch with her new friends in the café, and made headway on the kilt for Hugh. The only time she saw him was through his office window, when she was leaving the mill in the evening. He sat at his desk in front of the computer, his back to her.

At the castle, she ate alone except for the hounds, who looked longingly at her smoked haddock flan, left by Mrs. McNabb. While Sophie sat in front of her therapy lamp, she felt pretty sorry for herself. She missed Hugh…his lips and his companionship. When she trudged off to bed, though, she found a vase on Hugh's dresser with a note propped in front of it.

For Sophie:
Fiat Lux
(Let there be light)

"It's so beautiful!" she exclaimed to the Wallace and the Bruce. They weren't particularly impressed, barely raising their heads from where they rested on the master's bed.

She carefully picked up the vase, running her hands over the smooth exterior. It was all luminous blues and greens that seemed to shimmer with an internal light source, which reminded her of a loch with a sun at the bottom.

"I can't believe he did this." But Sophie had known for a long time what a good heart Hugh had. Amy had told her what had happened when her parents had died. Hugh had sat quietly with Amy after the funeral, knowing she simply needed him there, not to talk, but to understand.

Sophie replaced the vase, readied for bed, then retrieved her Gandiegow Fishing Village wall-hanging quilt from Hugh's chair, prepared to work on the binding. When she was done, she held it up, admiring the finished product, happy with how it turned out. Maybe she should leave it here for Hugh, a reminder of her. She spread the quilt over his cedar chest at the foot of the bed. When she climbed under the covers, she gave one last glance at her vase, a gift from the Laird before turning out the light.

Much later, when she heard Hugh in the room next to hers—and was sure he was asleep for the night—she crawled in next to him. She wrapped her arm around his waist and pressed her lips to his back.

"Thank you," she whispered.

He didn't wake up. She cuddled close and fell asleep.

The next three days passed pretty much the same, except there were no surprises waiting for Sophie on Hugh's dresser. She longed for time with the Laird, but it felt like she really was spending the week alone. Apparently, Hugh had gone on a hunger strike, disdaining to eat lunch with her again. *Or dinner.* Her time at the wool mill had turned precious, as she had grown very fond of the other workers she'd met. Willoughby had softened toward her, too, and Magnus was nothing but a big marshmallow under his crusty exterior.

Friday arrived too quickly, Sophie's last day. She stood at her workplace in the kiltmaker's shop, knowing she would miss the wool mill terribly when she went home tomorrow. Across the table from Willoughby, she picked up her scissors and trimmed the threads on the Laird's kilt, thinking about her quiet evenings at the castle this past week.

Aunt Davinia must've left the country, because Sophie hadn't seen or heard from her. Amy still wasn't taking her calls or answering her texts. When bedtime rolled around at Kilheath Castle, Sophie would stretch out in Hugh's king-size bed with her two four-legged friends. She smiled because her hearing had become as acute as the hounds'; for when Hugh slipped into his sister's room late that night, Sophie would go sleep with him one last time.

She'd started out sleeping with him to give *him* comfort, but cuddling him had become a comfort for *her*, too. Now she yearned for more. She loved cuddling up against him, but she was starting to feel rejected...though, to be fair, he always rested his arm over hers and held her hand in his sleep.

He hadn't kissed her since Sunday, and he hadn't laid a hand on her consciously—*either above her sweater or underneath it*. She was losing her one chance to make love to Hugh McGillivray, a chance of a lifetime, but she had a plan for tonight.

Tonight, she'd be brazen. It was no longer about losing her virginity, or being properly shagged before she left tomorrow evening. She truly cared for the Laird.

"Lass?" Willoughby barked from across the table. "Did ye not hear me? Damned daydreaming again. What's got into ye this afternoon?"

"Nothing," Sophie said, smiling at the old fellow. "I'll

miss ye, is all."

"Well, grab that buckle over there and get to sewing it in place."

"I thought Mrs. Bates sews on all the buckles. You said that she was the only one beside yereself that you trust to do it right." Sophie held a swatch of tartan over her heart. She'd found a place in this old man's shop, and she'd grown comfortable enough to goad him a little.

"Don't be cheeky with me," he rattled. "It would serve the Laird right to have his kilt fall off because of an ill-placed buckle. The man never should've stuck me with ye. Now get to sewing."

Sophie put down the scissors and hugged the old dear. "Ye'll miss me, too, won't ye?" She kissed his cheek.

The poor man was so stunned that he froze for a good ten seconds. He finally sighed, his shoulders sagging. "It will be quieter here without ye. Do you need help with where to place the damned buckle?"

"Aye. That would be grand." Though Sophie had seen Mrs. Bates put on enough buckles to know precisely what to do.

Willoughby spent the next five minutes instructing her on proper buckle placement and another five telling her the importance of using good strong thread and small stitches for this part of the process.

At five o'clock, he brought out tissue paper and a box for the Laird's completed kilt.

"Take it on up to the big house and show the Laird what ye've made."

She doubted Hugh would be home for dinner again tonight. She thanked Willoughby for everything and hugged him one last time before he locked up the workshop.

"Good luck to ye, lass." He patted her on the shoulder awkwardly. "Ye're a fine seamstress, and ye'll make some man very happy someday when ye get married."

Sophie adjusted Willoughby's scarf and then walked away, holding the box with the Laird's kilt inside. She couldn't concern herself with marriage any longer, but she intended to make one man very happy tonight.

***

Hugh was well aware that Sophie was going home tomorrow. Part of him couldn't wait to get his life back to normal—where he could concentrate on something more than the lovely body that snuggled up to him every night—and another part of him wanted to roar at the thought of her leaving.

Every night with Sophie's arms around him, more and more memories had come back—showering his consciousness, bathing him with goodness. *Happy memories.* Memories of his family and how they'd loved each other.

He hadn't slept on Chrissa's floor only after her death. He'd slept there even before the accident, every Christmas Eve from the time she was a baby, reading her *'Twas the Night Before Christmas* before she went to sleep.

He remembered the times he'd spent at the wool mill while learning the operation from his parents, knowing they were proud of him.

And he remembered their family meals. He'd

forgotten how happy they'd all been together, and now, somehow with Sophie cuddled up against him, he could remember the good and forget the bad.

Hugh turned out the light in his office, locked up, and left, thinking to surprise Sophie by being home for dinner. He'd called Mrs. McNabb earlier and asked her to leave them a supper which included haggis potato apple tarts. His cook had gone silent for a second, but she didn't question his choice. It was his favorite, and he hadn't asked for it since his sister's death.

All his staff and the whole town knew he had a house-guest, and he was sure the grapevine had been speculating...one of the reasons he'd put in long hours this week. Aunt Davinia had left him a note.

Urgent business in London and apologies for leaving poor Sophie to the gossip.

I'm sure you can make it right by the lass, and do something to salvage her reputation.

Auntie was as subtle as a bulldozer.

He rushed home, looking forward to surprising Sophie with a nice dinner. He wasn't trying to make it romantic, but he did have Mrs. McNabb set the grand dining room for their meal. He hoped she'd found the candlesticks that had been packed away long ago. He walked a little faster.

As he rounded the last bend, something caught his attention out of the corner of his eye. The outside light was on, and part of the loch was illuminated. Hugh heard Sophie's voice, speaking quietly, calmly, before he actually saw her.

"It's okay, boy, I'm coming out to get ye. Stay calm." Sophie's arms were in front of her, and she was shuffling her way out to the middle of the loch.

"Holy fuck!" he whispered. His mouth went dry, taking in the horror scene. One of his hounds, struggled to swim in the center through the broken ice. The other whined at the edge. And Sophie was heading to her certain death.

The Bruce, standing at the shore, sniffed the air, saw him, and began barking. Hugh took off at a dead run.

"Sophie," he yelled. "Don't move." *I'm coming.*

She glanced up, but didn't acknowledge his warning. She kept talking to the Wallace as she crouched down to lie on the ice.

Good girl. She knew to distribute her weight.

He was close, so close. But as she inched toward the struggling Wallace, he heard the ice cracking, a sound so familiar in his memory that it jarred his bones. *The sound of death.*

He couldn't get there in time. Just as she reached for the Wallace, the ice crumbled, and she went in, too.

Oh my God, not again! He ran to the edge of the loch, but stopped short. He wouldn't make the same mistake twice. "Hold on, Sophie," he said gruffly. God, he hated leaving her. But he ran full-out for the ghillie's shed and the rope hanging inside. He grabbed Chrissa's sled off the wall, too.

Back outside, he saw she had the Wallace in a death grip in one arm and struggled to tread water with the other.

As he rushed back to the ice, he tied the rope to the sled.

"Are ye okay?" He read somewhere that talking to the victim could help keep them calm. "I'm on my way."

"Hurry," she said breathlessly.

He slid the sled out to her. "I need ye to grab on to this." He hoped her hands weren't too frozen.

"I'll try." When it reached her, she got a hold of it, but it slipped from her hand.

"Again, Sophie." He couldn't lose her!

"I don't know if I can."

"Ye'll do it for me. For the Wallace. And for the Bruce." The Bruce dog was still barking encouragement from the shore. "Grab on to it because we need ye, lass," his heart pleaded.

His words energized her. This time when she grabbed the sled, she held on, gritting her chattering teeth. "P-pull, dammit," she growled.

Hugh hauled on the rope. The weight of the wet dog, Sophie, and her wet clothes was more than he'd expected. The Bruce barked more.

"Help, ye stupid mutt."

The Bruce ran for the end of the rope, gripped it in his teeth, and tugged. Sophie and the Wallace came out of the water.

"Ye're a damned good dog," Hugh grunted as he pulled. They weren't out of danger yet. It took everything in him not to run out and help her the rest of the way, but he kept tugging until at last he had her.

"I'm cold," she said through chattering teeth.

He picked her up and rushed for the house.

"What about the W-Wallace?" she whispered.

He glanced back. "He's coming. The Bruce is nudging him along."

Hugh took her into the house, the dogs following, and straight up to his room. He flipped the switch on the gas fireplace to warm the interior and headed to the en suite bathroom. He turned on the towel warmer with one hand before stepping into the Roman shower, fully clothed with Sophie still in his arms. He turned on the water, letting the spray wash over them.

"We don't want the water too hot," he explained calmly. His darling Sophie was shaking so. "I promise this'll raise your temperature." He carefully set her on the stone bench with water cascading over her. "I'm going to take yere wet things off so we can get the warm water to your skin."

"O-k-kay."

While he steadied her with his body, he pulled off her boots and socks. Then he undid her waterlogged coat and removed it.

"Ye know, lass, many times this past week," he said, trying to give her a playful smile, "I've imagined peeling yere clothes off ye, though never under these circumstances."

She gave him a valiant smile, but shivered violently, sputtering when water got in her mouth. "I hope I don't drown first."

"Ye're my braw lass." He laughed, knowing it was a

good sign that she was spouting off at him at a time like this. "Come on. Let's get this sweater off of you. Ye can leave on yere bra." He eased it over her head as her next sentence registered.

"I'm not wearing one." And she wasn't.

"Oh, God." He thought he might hyperventilate. "Ye're beautiful, lass."

"Ye're just hard up." Her teeth chattered with her arms plastered at her sides.

He kissed her. He couldn't help himself—he was such a bastard to take advantage of her. But she kissed him back, melting into him as he held her tightly.

"Oh, Sophie, I don't know what I would've done—" He broke off.

She shh'ed him. "It's o-okay, Hugh. I'm okay."

Fortunately, the way he was holding her kept her from seeing his face. Raw emotions coursed through him— terror, anger, relief, and gratitude. Gradually, where cold and upset had been, only joy remained. They stayed like that for a long time, until she wasn't shaking nearly as much and he was feeling calmer.

Finally, he remembered his duty. "Let's get these pants off of ye, too."

"You f-first." A bit of laughter was in her voice.

"Oh, God, don't tell me that ye're not wearing any skivvies." He looked down, which was a huge mistake. Her wee perfect breasts were right there in his line of sight, and he was as hard as a rock.

"I'm wearing *skivvies,* as ye say. It's just that, ye know, they're not verra prim and proper." Her cheeks were pinking up nicely, a good sign she was going to be fine.

He brushed her cheek. "Well, close yere eyes, lass, so ye won't see *me* when I'm scandalized by yere under-things."

He didn't wait for her consent but undid her pants and pushed them down to her ankles.

"Step out." His voice was hoarse with his face inches away from the black lace of nothing that she wore. And God help him, he put his mouth over the small V and gave it a worshiping kiss. Before he did more, he rose. "How are ye feeling?"

"Do that again, and I'd be damned near on fire."

"Let's get you dried off and warmed up under the quilts." Keeping his boxers on, Hugh stripped out of his soaked shirt and slacks, leaving them and Sophie in the running water while he toweled off. He dressed in fleece pants before grabbing two warm towels from the rack.

He turned off the shower, swaddled Sophie in the towels, and carried her to his room. For once, the Wallace and the Bruce weren't on the bed, but were in front of the fireplace. The Bruce was lying up against the Wallace, licking his ear.

Hugh pulled back the covers with one hand while he set Sophie down. "Slip off those panties so yere bed won't get wet." He wanted to do it himself, but was pretty certain he wouldn't be able to stop what he wanted to do next.

"*My* bed?" She looked at him incredulously. "Where are ye going?"

"Don't worry, lass," he chuckled. "I'll be right back." He went to the en suite and grabbed the other warmed towels and wrapped them around the Wallace.

He hurried back to the bed and pulled her into his arms, knowing the skin-to-skin contact was a good way to keep her warm. He tried *not* to think about her being naked, but she kept nibbling at his neck.

He looked up at the ceiling at the crack that had formed the year Chrissa died. It was past time to fix it. "I want to thank you."

She stopped in mid-nibble. "For what?"

"For lying next to me these last several nights." *For helping me to remember my family in a good light.*

She pulled away.

"So ye were awake?" Her words were filled with hurt and disbelief. "The whole time?"

"Aye."

She sat up, scooting away from him. "Ye pretended to be asleep, because what? I was too plain to have in yere bed?"

He pulled her back into his arms and kissed the top of her head. "Calm yereself, woman."

"I'm going home tomorrow," she whispered angrily. "I don't want to go home a virgin."

"Nay. Ye're staying here with me. I mean to make you my wife." He'd made the decision subconsciously while she'd held him night after night. He couldn't ever let her go.

The word *virgin* finally sank into Hugh's brain. "Ye're a what?

6

"YE MEAN TO MAKE ME YERE WIFE?" So-
phie's voice was shrill. Water must still be in her
ears. Or the chill had cracked her brain.

"I'm finally going to do as Amy and Aunt Davinia bid
me to do." He looked confused—like he was saying one
thing while puzzling over another. "They've nagged me to
marry you for the last year, and now I will."

An arrow pierced straight through Sophie's heart. Not
one of Cupid's arrows either.

Something was very wrong with what he was saying.
She had liked Hugh even before she'd met him. Amy's
stories about Hugh and their misadventures as children
and young adults had painted him in the most lovable

light. When Sophie had seen him for the first time, she'd been instantly attracted to him, though he'd been a prat.

Then somewhere along the line in the last week, she'd fallen hopelessly in love with Hugh McGillivray, the flesh-and-blood man. The real deal. Perhaps it had happened when they were isolated at the cabin and he'd shared his deepest, darkest secret with her so she would know she wasn't alone in her pain. Or maybe while she'd been holding him night after night while he lay next to his dead sister's bed. Hell, as hard up as she was, she'd probably fallen in love with him on the first night…when she'd seen him naked.

Shouldn't she feel grateful to him that he'd given in to his relations' hounding and had agreed to marry the *unmarriageable Sophie?*

Except she couldn't marry him if he felt forced into it!

"Get me some pajamas," she said coolly, pushing away from him. "I need my cell phone, too." Being demanding was better than crying.

"Ye don't need pajamas." His voice was as hard as the ice on the loch should have been.

"I do. And don't forget the phone." She was going home—now. She wasn't going to inflict herself on him any longer.

Hugh had a bemused expression on his face as he rolled out of bed. He pulled his pajama top from the closet and retrieved her cell from the dresser.

"Here." He left her with the things and went into the loo.

Sophie couldn't tell him the truth. It was too painful. If only he wanted her for the right reasons!

She would not crumple into a heap. Not now. She started to call home, but no way did Sophie want to be stuck in a car with Mama questioning her all the way back to Gandiegow. Sophie pulled on Hugh's pajama top and dialed her cousin, the one person who wouldn't badger her to death about what had happened and how she was feeling.

"Ramsay, it's me, Sophie. I need ye to come and get me," she said, starting to shake, and not from the cold either.

"Give me the address," Ramsay said. "I'll leave now."

She gave him the directions and hung up. She looked up and found Hugh standing in the doorway.

"What's this about?" he said roughly.

The dogs raised their heads and gave her a questioning stare. They all waited for her answer. She didn't have the energy to speak. It had been a harrowing evening—she'd not used her therapy lamp—and the depression was swallowing her and taking her words with it.

"Ye're not going anywhere," he said.

Sophie didn't meet his eyes, but went to the dresser and scooped out her panties, laying them on the comforter. Hugh's eyes flashed with desire at her slutty undies, but then his glare went icy cold in the next second.

She went to the third drawer and pulled out a turtleneck, jeans, and a sweater. She opened her mouth to tell him to step out of the room while she dressed, but he'd already seen all she had—maybe even seen to her very soul. She had a moment of gumption as she pulled his pajama top over her head like she was a snake shedding its skin. *A new woman.* Naked, but with a new determination. She silently dared Hugh to say something as she put on a warm turtleneck.

He glared at her with his hands on his hips. "What has got into you?"

"Nothing's got into me." Amy and Aunt Davinia would have to come up with a new bride for Hugh to wed. *And bed.*

But underneath it all…Sophie was amazed that during Hugh's non-proposal—somewhere, somehow—she'd found her own worth.

She didn't have to marry to feel like a whole person.

He grabbed her arm. "Talk to me, dammit. Don't shut me out." He paused for a second as if the answer had occurred to him. He dropped her arm and stepped back. "Do ye need time in front of yere lamp?"

The question knocked the air out of her.

She grabbed a pillow and threw it at his head, wishing for more—like a club to use on his thick skull.

He'd done her a favor with his last words, reminding her that she was damaged, defective, giving her just enough energy to go. She jammed all her clothes into her suitcase. She looked mournfully at the vase. She couldn't keep it without thinking of him. She left the vase sitting on his dresser…and her Gandiegow wallhanging over the cedar chest. It would serve him right for pieces of her to remain behind. As she wheeled her bag to exit, he stood in the doorway, blocking it.

"Don't," he said through clenched teeth.

But he was settling. He didn't *want* to marry her; he'd made that clear. Ultimately, he was only going to marry because his family wished him to. The Laird may not love her, but Sophie had finally figured out that she loved herself.

She pushed past him. "Come, boys, walk me downstairs." The Wallace and the Bruce followed her down, one towel staying on the Wallace until he hit the final step.

Sophie went into the parlor, wishing she could make a quick getaway, but Ramsay wouldn't arrive for some time. She threw a log on the fire for the hounds, and then sat at the writing desk to do some light therapy as she waited.

The longer she sat in front of her lamp, the sadder she felt. She was going home defeated and would live with her parents for the rest of her life. The truth was, she would miss being at Kilheath Castle, miss holding the Laird while he slept.

She loved Hugh—there was no denying it—she only wished he loved her back. She wiped away a tear. And just in time, too.

Hugh brought a tray in and set it down on the coffee table.

"Eat," he said. "Drink. Refuel." He didn't seem capable of full sentences.

Sophie turned off her lamp, unplugged it, and carefully wound up the cord. She put it with her other things by the parlor entrance before walking to the tray, all the fight gone from her. She grabbed a tart and the mug of tea.

He pointed to the loveseat. "Sit."

She couldn't relax as she had on her first day here, when she'd pretended to be queen of the castle. All those illusions had been vanquished. The dogs came to lie next to her as if they didn't want to miss one second of her being there either. As the time ticked away, Hugh seemed to inch closer to her, also.

After a long while, he sighed heavily as if the fight was all gone from him, too. "Ye have to tell me what happened. Ye owe me at least that before ye go."

A sharp rap sounded at the front door. For a second, Hugh kept staring at her like he hadn't heard.

The knock came again, longer and harder. Hugh stomped off toward the foyer.

What could Sophie say to the Laird? When he'd declared that he'd marry her, he'd said nothing of love.

Sharp voices from the hallway interrupted her regrets. *Crap.* Maybe having Ramsay fetch her had been stupid. Mama would've been better.

Sophie grabbed her luggage as she hurried from the parlor. The dogs popped up and followed. She found Hugh in the foyer, standing nose-to-nose with Ramsay.

"What's this?" Hugh said to her accusingly.

Sophie could've cleared things up and mentioned Ramsay was her cousin, but she wanted to hurt Hugh, like he'd done to her.

"He's my ride."

***

Hugh wanted to punch the bloke in the jaw. He remembered him—*Ramsay*, Amy had called him. He was from Gandiegow. Hugh had seen him at the céilidh last summer. Where Hugh had acted the stubborn prat. He should've danced with Sophie. He should've made her his then.

Hugh stepped into Sophie's path. "Ye don't have to do this, lass."

The Wallace and the Bruce each rubbed up against her, also presenting their arguments as to why she should stay.

Ramsay looked to Sophie. "What is it? Stay or go?"

"I'm ready." She sounded sad, but determined.

The bloke grabbed her bag and her lamp. For a moment, Hugh thought Ramsay might give them a moment to say good-bye in private, but the bastard just stood there, waiting for Sophie to go out first.

Hugh reached for her, but she sidestepped him and fled into the night.

Ramsay shrugged. "The lass has made her decision." And he was gone, too, closing the door behind them.

Hugh punched the wall, barely feeling the bruising of his knuckles. The dogs whined. The Wallace went to the door and scratched at the ancient entry, barking. The Bruce began to howl.

"Enough," Hugh yelled, but it did no good.

"What's all this racket?" Aunt Davinia said, coming in from the kitchen. "I stopped by to borrow some clotted cream for tomorrow morning's scone and find this.

Where's Sophie?"

The dogs ran to his aunt as if to tattle.

She glared at him sideways. "What did ye do, Hugh-boy?"

He ran a hand through his hair. "I didn't do anything. I told Sophie she was going to be my wife, and she couldn't be rid of me fast enough."

He didn't add that she'd left with another man. Hugh wanted to howl like the dogs.

Auntie snapped her fingers, and both beasts sat, as if turned to porcelain. She narrowed her gaze on Hugh. "So did ye tell the lass that ye've finally come to yere senses, that ye love her?"

"She didn't exactly give me the chance."

"No, ye didn't give *her* a chance," his aunt said. "She needed to hear it from you, how ye feel about her, the words from yere heart. What did ye do? Did ye just tell her how it was going to be? Of course that's what ye did!"

She motioned to the Wallace and the Bruce. "Dammit, Hugh, she's not one of the hounds. She wants to be asked. She wants to be wooed. She wants to be cherished." Auntie shook her head with more disappointment than he'd ever seen from her. "Get off yere arse and go after her. Do it right now, for goodness' sake."

He started to argue. But, dammit, it didn't matter that Ramsay might be a towering, warrior of a Scot, Hugh's equal. Hugh had something greater going for him. He loved Sophie!

"Come on, Wallace. Ye, too, Bruce. We're going after

the mistress of the castle."

***

Sophie cried silently in the darkness as Ramsay drove. As she'd expected, she didn't have to explain anything to him.

Back home in Gandiegow, though, Sophie couldn't dodge her mama's scrutiny. Annie hovered and clucked, made her a cup of tea, and sat with her on the couch. At Mama's insistence, Da came in and sat with them, too.

Sophie didn't tell them anything, though Annie had tried every trick in the book to get her to spill it.

"Ye talk to her, Russ. She needs to tell us what happened so we can help her." Annie patted her on the hand, and then glared at Sophie's da.

Da leaned forward, giving Sophie a look of understanding. "Ye don't have to tell us a thing. Ye only need to give me the nod, and I'll give Hugh McGillivray a visit he won't soon forget."

Sophie loved these people, but she was done being their troubled daughter. "Nay. It's not Hugh's fault. It's me."

"What do ye mean it's yere fault? Nighean, ye're perfect," Annie said.

Sophie considered hurling her mug at the hearth, but it was Mama's favorite. "You and I know I'm far from perfect."

Maybe it was time for some gut-wrenching honesty between her and her parents. "I heard you and Da speaking before I left to housesit at Hugh's."

Her mother looked at her, confused. "About what?"

Da grabbed a fishing magazine from the coffee table and leaned back in his recliner.

Just as he was opening the pages, Sophie jumped in with both feet. "I heard you two agree that I was past my prime. Too old to find anyone. Too bossy."

Da dropped his magazine, straightening back up, his attention on her. "What are ye talking about, hen? I never..." His voice trailed off.

Mama stared at Da, very serious-like. "No."

The two of them burst out laughing, Annie clutching Sophie's da.

"I don't see anything funny here," Sophie said. *This day had gone from bad to worse.*

Mama calmed a little and patted Sophie's arm. "Ye got it all wrong. We were speaking of Deydie, not you."

"Da, what's Mama talking about?" Sophie asked.

Her father pulled out a wrinkled handkerchief and dabbed at his eyes. He shoved it back into his pocket. "Yere mama and the other ladies of Gandiegow think ol' Deydie and Abraham Clacher would make a fine couple. But, good grief, I don't see it. That woman is too old and crotchety, and Abraham is too salty of a fisherman, for those two"—he chuckled again—"for those two to get married."

"See, nighean, we weren't talking about ye after all. Ye just misheard."

Sophie didn't have time to process the revelation as

someone started pounding on the door. She went to answer it. Ramsay stood there, but then the Wallace and the Bruce tore past him in a blur and jumped on her.

They would've knocked her over, too, if two strong arms hadn't caught her. It wasn't Ramsay who held her either.

"Down, boys," Hugh said. Ramsay had been shoved to the side.

Ramsay tipped an imaginary hat at Hugh. "My work here is done." Then Ramsay was gone.

Hugh shut the door behind him, still holding on to her, keeping the dogs at bay—sort of. Based on the way he was holding her, he wasn't letting go.

The laughter in the living room had come to a complete halt. Da rose and came to stand near Sophie. Hugh wrapped a protective arm around her—or was that a possessive arm?—and pulled her tightly against his side.

"Do I need to have a talk here with yere young man, daughter?" Da was an inch shorter than Hugh, but her da was giving him a glare that would've had a lesser man running for the door.

"I'd introduce myself, sir, but apparently ye already know who I am," Hugh said respectfully, but firmly. "May I speak with yere daughter alone?"

Da looked to Sophie, and she nodded.

"I'll leave ye be," her father said. "For now. But the second she's done with ye, ye better let her out of your grasp." He glared at the hand that gripped her shoulder.

"Sophie, we'll be in our room, if ye need us." Mama

took Da's hand and led him away.

Sophie broke free and went to the couch. The dogs went with her, climbing up, each laying their heads in her lap.

"What do you want, Hugh? I heard all I needed to hear back at yere castle."

A strange thought hit Sophie. If she'd been wrong about her parents and what they thought of her, maybe she was wrong about Hugh, too. She scratched the Bruce behind the ears as he groaned.

She kept her gaze down as Hugh walked into the living room and sat in her da's recliner. She did a double take. He was wearing the kilt she'd made for him.

"There are things I failed to say." His voice was a hoarse whisper.

The emotion behind his words forced her to peek at him. He sat forward, making the old recliner creak and looked vulnerable. She wanted to go to him and put her arms around him, but she couldn't…not until she was certain why he'd chased her through the night and what he'd come to say.

He leaned closer. "I got the order all screwed up."

"That doesn't make any sense." And it wasn't what she wanted to hear.

He cleared his throat and swallowed. "I should've told ye how much ye've come to mean to me, Sophie Munro."

The Wallace yawned loudly and stretched further across her lap.

She wanted to say, *And?* Because her traitorous heart

was impatient and hopeful that Hugh really did care for her.

He took her hand. "I should've told ye that I loved yere arms being wrapped around me night after night."

Da harrumphed loudly from the other room.

Hugh glanced in that direction, but soldiered on. "I'm not afraid of the dark anymore. I haven't had a nightmare all week. But most of all, ye helped me to remember all the wonderful things in life—past, present, and future. Ye've healed me." He kissed her palm. "I should've told ye that I love ye. Ye made me whole again, lass, and I'd be a fool not to claim ye as mine for always."

Mama's "ahhh" slipped from under their bedroom door.

Hugh got down on his knee and took Sophie's other hand from the Wallace. "Please say that ye'll marry me, Sophie."

"Down, boys," she commanded, and for a second, Hugh pulled back. "Not you. You stay."

She fell to her knees and wrapped her arms around him, hugging him. Mama and Da started to bicker in the other room. Sophie didn't get a chance to answer Hugh before Mama burst through her bedroom door, dragging Da behind her.

"So what did ye say?" Her mother stopped short at the sight of Sophie and Hugh kneeling on her living room floor, arms around each other. "Oh. Then ye've told the lad yes?"

Sophie got to her feet, pulling Hugh to his as well. Da,

blushing and looking uncomfortable, was tugging Mama's hand, trying to get her to go back to the bedroom with him. But Mama wasn't budging.

Da shot Sophie a look. "Answer the lad, daughter, so yere mother and me can be off to bed."

Sophie turned to Hugh and gazed into his lovely brown eyes.

"Aye, I'll marry ye. But on one condition."

Both of her parents gasped at her audacity.

Sophie ignored them. "I'll marry ye as long as ye'll always kiss me as ye do now."

"Aye," Hugh vowed.

She pushed his hair away from his eyes—eyes that held *love for her*. "Ye've become my sunshine in the darkness. Did ye know that?"

"And ye've become mine as well."

Hugh kissed her then, and the world spun deliciously out of control, making her dizzy with joy. When she opened her eyes sometime later, she was settled on the couch, her parents were off to bed for the night, and the Wallace and the Bruce were asleep in front of the fire.

And the Laird? Well, he was right where she wanted him. He was in her arms, nibbling on her ear, making plans about their life to come, all in that voice of his that had her melting a hundred different ways.

"And ye'll always be mine, Sophie," he declared.

She smiled obediently. "Aye. I know. Because the Laird says so."

"Nay. Because ye're a treasure. And I'm going to

spend the rest of my life making ye the happiest woman alive."

And he did.

If you enjoyed reading this book, please *recommend* it to your friends or your book club. And please *write a review*. Readers love them and authors depend on them. If you write a review for *Blame It on Scotland,* please let me know. I would like to **thank you** personally.

Email: **patience@patiencegriffin.com**

For Signed copies, visit:

www.PatienceGriffin.com

JOIN Patience's Newsletter!
...to find out about events, contests, and more!

www.PatienceGriffin.com

A
Kilts & Quilts®
Novel

BOOKS by
PATIENCE GRIFFIN

KILTS AND QUILTS SERIES:
ROMANTIC WOMEN'S FICTION

#1   *TO SCOTLAND WITH LOVE*

#2   *MEET ME IN SCOTLAND*

#3   *SOME LIKE IT SCOTTISH*

#4   *THE ACCIDENTAL SCOT*

#5   *THE TROUBLE WITH SCOTLAND*

#6   *IT HAPPENED IN SCOTLAND*

#6.5 *THE LAIRD AND I*

#7   *BLAME IT ON SCOTLAND*

#8   *KILT IN SCOTLAND*

Other books by Patience:

To Scotland with Love

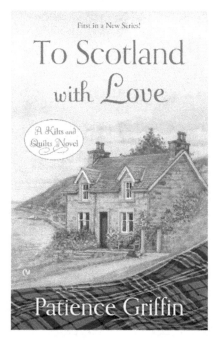

Welcome to the charming Scottish seaside town of Gandiegow—where two people have returned home for different reasons, but to find the same thing....

Caitriona Macleod gave up her career as an investigative reporter for the role of perfect wife. But after her husband is found dead in his mistress's bed, a devastated Cait leaves Chicago for the birthplace she hasn't seen since she was a child. She's hoping to heal and to reconnect with her gran. The last thing she expects to find in Gandiegow is the Sexiest Man Alive! She just may have stumbled on the ticket to reigniting her career—if her heart doesn't get in the way.

Graham Buchanan is a movie star with many secrets. A Gandiegow native, he frequently hides out in his hometown between films. He also has a son he'll do anything to protect. But Cait Macleod is too damn appealing—even if she is a journalist.

Quilting with her gran and the other women of the village brings Cait a peace she hasn't known in years. But if she turns in the story about Graham, Gandiegow will never forgive her for betraying one of its own. Should she suffer the consequences to resurrect her career? Or listen to her battered and bruised heart and give love another chance?

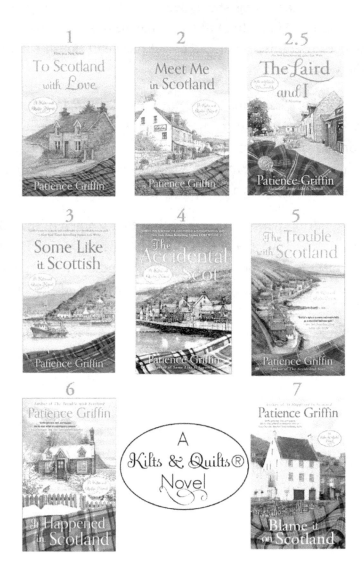